THE TEXAS GUN

Sheep were on the move and the tempers of hard-pressed cowmen were on the rise. Drought had hit them hard, losses were high, and being sheeped out would ruin them completely.

For reasons of their own, the U.S. Forestry Service wanted trouble stirred up between the beef riders and the mutton punchers. They figured it would force Congress to give them what they were after. And they thought they had their trouble-maker in the escaped killer, Pete McGrath.

Raising Cain came easy to McGrath—gun battles, fist fights, grass-burning and hoorawing honest folks were second nature to him. But this time even McGrath didn't realise just how much hell-raising would be needed to take him off the Foresters' hook.

THE TEXAS GUN

Nelson Nye

GUNSMOKE

First published in the UK by Jenkins

This hardback edition 2006
by BBC Audiobooks Ltd
by arrangement with
Golden West Literary Agency

ISBN 1 4056 8069 5

British Library Cataloguing in Publication Data available.

Printed and bound in Great Britain by
Antony Rowe Ltd., Chippenham, Wiltshire

I

Peering down at the town from the western slope of these rock strewn Mazatzals—half hidden in the shade of ancient sycamores where it sprawled along the dry bed of a creek—I supposed folks would wonder what trouble had fetched me to so bedraggled a jumping-off place as Sunflower.

Not that it made any great amount of difference.

There would always be those, no matter where a man went, bound to pick and to pry with stares slanched from blank faces, getting their wind up while biding their chance to shove a spoke through his wheel. It was always the same, an old and hateful pattern filled with twists and turns leading inevitably to the time when departure would look the better part of valor.

Nobody with any working parts in his think-box was going to take me for any chuck-line rider. The look of my gear, the rig I had under me, bore marks to be read, and no amount of whiskers or other makeshift dodges was like to brush over my Texas way of talking.

I had a right to feel nervous. It was a poor time of year to come into strange country with crews all settled into their jobs and calf roundup just over. No one was like to be hiring here now and without any reason for hanging around I was going to stand out like the side of a mountain.

Though still a good piece as the horse had to go, I considered the town for another ten minutes, trying to make up my mind. A man in my boots didn't have many choices, not if his intention was to stay in the quick.

If I pushed right along I could be there by sundown. The only travel I'd seen since passing through Globe were the lifts of dust which occasionally spun across empty troughs between this tumbled chaos of hills. Three-four times I'd caught glimpses of the headquarters buildings of faraway ranches. Only rider I saw in all those miles was a steeple-hatted ranahan on a mouse-colored hide. Flashes of silver had shone for a moment as this gent hauled around to sheer off on a course calculated to make certain I wouldn't get within gun-shot without I deliberately set out to do so. No one but a plumb fool would try that.

Just before I got down off the mountain—probably still the best part of ten miles from town, a pattern of dust shaped up on the right. It was pretty soon plain that somebody—maybe several—was aiming to flank me.

I didn't take to this kindly but it soon became evident there was just the one horse. I still didn't like it. This could be the same ranny who had hauled off before, come back to have a look—or it could be someone else with a new set of notions. Whoever it was it looked like he figured on pacing me in.

I hadn't come this far to take needless chances.

I dropped off my horse keeping hold of the reins. Without loosening the cinches I squatted down in the shade of a scrawny mesquite and rolled up a smoke to ease off my hunger.

The way anyone will with long distances to cover, I'd been taking pretty good care of this horse. While he didn't look fresh he hadn't been pushed and could still throw a burst of speed if he had to. I'd have felt a mite easier with rifle in hand but it wouldn't have looked friendly if that dust-maker yonder should happen to ride over to see what had become of me.

When I'd finished my smoke and he still hadn't come, I got up, put a heel on it and got back in the saddle. I sat there a moment still thinking about it, pushing it around like a cat with a spool, not exactly nervous, not really satisfied either. In strange country it paid a man to stay on his toes.

I went on, but careful, plenty alert to the sounds and sights that came within my ken. I saw everything that was there to be seen, not happy at all with this disquieting stillness. I'm a man that likes birds to chatter. When I see them sitting like vultures on a limb, with never a peep for a man riding by, it generally tends to aggravate my hackles.

This continuing silence pushed a mort of dark thoughts through the crannies of my mind.

But nothing untoward occurred to further alarm me. There were no more dusts and, if anyone was laying out to follow my progress, the stares I chucked at the most likely places failed to turn up any evidence of it.

Sunflower was no metropolis. It was hardly more than a bulge in the road running north from Phoenix to Payson and Strawberry, crossing the Verde as it left Tonto Basin through as wild a stretch of owlhoot country as a man could hope to find in those days. Which was why, in a way, I had been pointed toward it.

The town had grown up round a general store that existed to supply local outfits and such masterless men holed up in the hills as the cut-and-run killers, bank robbers and rustlers run out of more settled communities.

It had one hotel—this one. Upon the commode holding washbowl and pitcher—beside which I'd been hunkered a slack-muscled—stood a bottle, a tumbler and a ripped-open envelope. On the wall looking back at me a faded and fly-spotted colored print showed an artist's conception of the Battle of Picacho Peak, about the only real fracas Donophan got into.

Tired and disgusted, I was in a bad mood. It was 6:15 when I'd picked up the bottle, and the message in the envelope they'd been holding at the desk. The gods could have their laugh. Gold Spur Charlie, while I'd been riding all those goddam miles, had stopped a knife in a barroom brawl two hundred miles east of here at Luna, in the San Francisco Mountains.

Now the bottle was two-thirds empty. Four hours trying to wash the taste of it out of me, and all I'd to show for that brainless performance was the same wild fury I had felt to begin with.

I sure as hell wasn't drunk. I was, however, suddenly conscious of the heat. The room was hot as the nethermost hinges. I was clammy with sweat as I pushed to my feet, wheeling toward the shut window on legs that seemed filled with needles and pins. An impatient jerk sent it rattling up. Summer smell and town stinks came in to mingle with the stuffy stench of too many unwashed tenants before me. The night outside was unfathomably black as I stared toward unseen distant peaks.

I put my back to the window with a bitter oath, dragged the flat of a hand across damp cheeks. That woman in the next room was bawling again; not easily nor loud but with an anguished half-strangled gulping sound as though for something beyond human cure.

In the wall that was nearest—my own lamp was out —light filtered through those places where tongue-in-groove boards no longer met. "Back in ten minutes," a man's voice said gruffly. "Be ready."

Floorboards skreaked beneath his weight. A door was hauled open; slammed loudly behind him.

What ailed her was certainly no affair of mine. Crying, I'd noticed, came easy after marriage, whether a parson had blessed it or not. Some women took a deal of comfort from the process. This, for my money, was probably one of that kind.

I crossed the room, found the lamp in its bracket, lifted the chimney and dragged a match across its wick. I picked up the bottle, shook it, stood eyeing it. Put it back down. Drink was a fool's crutch; I'd been a-round enough to know that. Round enough to loathe the uneasy fawning that all too often came cheek by jowl with discovery of my identity.

Rebellious thoughts dived into the past, through turmoil I'd known to the name I had made synonymous with violence.

Yet what sort of choice had I ever been given?

Peter McGrath I'd been named in the note found pinned to the shawl-padded basket left on the steps of a foundling's home. It hadn't been that which had curdled my life, nor the couple of times I had climbed through a window to be fetched back and chastised for my trouble—that was deep in a past I seldom scanned.

The things I saw were those long dragged-out months of trickery and hate I had spent on a trail that had taken me into all kinds of back corners. Cow nursing, brush running, incredible weeks of hardships and dangers that seared like the bite of a white-hot iron. Jerky, beans and rancid coffee. Pounding hooves and breath-clogging peril, swinging ropes and sudden death, with ever before me the elusive shadow of the phantom that wouldn't be brought into focus.

These were what Charlie had taken me through and now the son of a bitch was dead—forever gone beyond my reach.

Killed in a bar brawl.

Jesus Christ!

I caught up my hat and jammed it on. With the irony

of it burning through me like acid, I had to get out of that goddam room. Strapping the shell belt about my waist was a thing of pure reflex; I've no remembrance of buckling it on. Two strides took my weight to the top of the stairs. A rumble of sound took me past the desk and a white-faced clerk I didn't half see. Then I was out in the trapped heat of the half railed veranda, shivering in the grip of my fury, no longer caring if I was recognized or not.

Every dodge I had tried—everything I had stood for —was toppled, meaningless shards underfoot. *How was a man to pick up the pieces of a life that no longer mattered to anyone?*

But old habits are not sluffed off so easily. The needs of survival had been ground hard into me. No sooner was I into the blue dark of that street than some sixth sense stopped me dead in my tracks.

I was hemmed by a quiet too thick for belief.

Four silent, and blanket wrapped shapes squatted shoulder to shoulder at the plank walk's edge. San Carlos Apaches! What the hell were they doing here?

I followed their stares across hoof tracked dust to the street's far side where, in the deeper black of a store's wooden awning, something moved fractionally.

I sucked in a breath as farther down my questing glance found another bit of motion. There was the pinpoint gleam of cigar or cigarette from the curdled gloom of a stable doorway. A fourth man, discovered beyond the butter-yellow shine of a lamplit window, sent bitter clamor through me.

Temper burned inside my guts with a fiercening intensity as one swift step took me out of their view beneath the veranda overhang. With hand half curled, I waited out the play, tipped forward, resting on the soles of spurred boots.

Across the way, a door swung abruptly open, its lance

of light cutting baldly aslant the ruts of the road. The glow from the stable smoker vanished and the quiet took on a new dimension as a man's emerging bulky length, crossing that shaft, turned hovering shadows more deeply black.

I knew in those breathless stretched-out seconds that he, not I, was the one being waited for, and settled more comfortably into my tracks.

But almost at once I tipped forward again, cursing myself for a stupid fool. What happened to him was no skin off my nose, but I understood—even as I told myself this—I couldn't just stand there and watch a man die. The fellow coming out of that lamplit doorway had on the uniform of the newly established Forest Service, which stood in its way for law and order—two things this country had long been in need of.

It was odd, I suppose, if you stopped to think back on it, that a gent who'd been bucking all kinds of law should suddenly feel any kinship with it. I knew right enough it was the worst kind of folly but I couldn't keep still with that scum laying for him. "Get back!" I shouted. "Get back inside!"

The echoes caromed off the street's false fronts and faded away in the creep of the heightened quiet's return. Not even a cricket's chirp came out of the gloom round my bunched muscles stance. The ranger had got himself out of the doorway. I saw no sign of those posted shapes.

I looked at the Indians limned in the shine from the hotel windows. They were stolidly there as four lumps carved from stone. If not completely indifferent, they at least knew enough to stay on their haunches and give that appearance. Only a fool bought chips in a game that didn't concern him.

I shrugged and sighed and, remounting the steps, to drown crowding thoughts went into the bar. I knew with a hot intolerance I'd better be shaking the dust of this burg. To stay on here after a play like that made about as much sense as a pulque drunk squaw.

I caught up the bottle the apron set out and poured a stiff jolt. Then stood a bit holding the glass left-handed, staring into the amber gleam of that bourbon, mirthlessly smiling as I remembered the message picked up at the desk. Charlie's death had left me with no place to go. It had cut loose a heap of things I'd have to get used to.

But old habits cling.

The barkeep had gone swirling his rag down the oak. I slanched a covert look into the mirror but no one was watching. Him and me, it appeared, had the place to ourselves. I put the glass down untasted, left a coin there beside it and wheeled through the bat-wings.

I was in no mood to play hide and seek. Crossing the veranda, I stepped into the street, passed through a crisscross of light and entered a hash house.

At this time of night it wasn't bursting with customers. On a stool at the counter a Mexican teamster folded over his plate was shoveling refried beans onto his fork with the half eaten taco he used for a pusher. Yonder, at one of the wallside tables, a man sat with a woman.

She kept her eyes on her eatables as I took the table next to them, walking round it to get into a chair that had its back to the wall. I gave the fat cook my order and he went back to his stove. When the food came I ate it, then sat back and rolled a smoke.

Though she kept staring into her plate as if oblivious to everything around her, she did not take much interest in eating. In a flushed sort of way I suppose you'd have called her pretty, with that piled-up mass of spun-gold hair, but her shape like her looks had probably seen better days. She was young enough still

—in her twenties I reckoned—but curves that once might have raised the old Adam were commencing to forecast a time when corsets would not be able to contain her.

The man, meal finished, was carefully twirling a cigar above the heat of a match. A soft-spoken gent with a college man's diction and a too handsome face that—considering the gloss of benchmade boots and the West Coast elegance of sporty clothes—suggested this was one who could be easily affronted. That he took himself real serious was plain as the chain that linked his hunting-case timepiece to the center topaz button of that flower-embroidered vest.

I suspected his companion was the woman I'd heard crying. He looked the kind who'd make a lot of women trouble.

She must have sensed my covert scrutiny. Green eyes came up with a kind of open challenge that forced my own away from her and left me feeling foolish.

I stubbed out my smoke and called across to the cook for another cup of java, not yet ready to step into that street and the prospect of what those four I had thwarted might have set up in the way of a welcome.

"Fetch a slab of pie, too," I called, and when the fat man put this order down in front of me, I handed him a bill and shoved the change in my pocket.

That wedge of pie looked as toothsome as something left from the days of Cain and Abel. I had picked up my fork and was irritably wondering if the knife perhaps might not be more practical, when the pair at the next table put their show on the road. The man had said something to her, something gruff I didn't catch. Now the woman yapped back. She had spunk, anyway —I'll give her that. She said with a resentful sharpness, "*I won't!* I won't go there with you, damn it, and you—"

The man didn't wait to hear the rest of it. He reached above their table and backhanded her across the face.

She came to her feet with a strangled cry, cheek red against white with the print of his hand. She looked pale and shaken, stood trembling, glaring with a fiercening defiance as he kicked back his chair. He had the hand half up when I said to him softly: "Don't reckon I'd try that again, was I you."

His shape swung completely around. Color livened the set of that too handsome face. His eyes were bright with a brashening outrage. His right fist dropped till the spraddling fingers were hardly an inch from the butt of the gun that was there beneath the flung-back skirt of his coat. "Get out!" he growled in a husky whisper. "*Git!*"

And started ominously toward me.

I stayed where I was. I hadn't even got up. I showed him my teeth in a saturnine grin.

The man stopped in his tracks. "What the bloody hell you laughing at?" he said in a voice like a rusty gate hinge.

"You," I told him. "You ain't scarin' nobody."

With a curse, his fingers closed round the gun. The sound of the shot in the confines of that room shook a pan off the wall somewhere back of the stove. The man's grabbed pistol, torn from his hand, jounced off a table and skittered over the floor. He crouched there, rooted, incredulously staring, then peered at the fingers of his shocked and tingling hand.

"You owe the lady an apology. She's waiting."

The dude's black look got purely wild. He flicked a wrist and a knife jumped out of that sleeve like a snake.

It was all the encouragement my temper needed. I took one forward step and struck. The blow caught this puke at the hinge of his jaw and drove him, gagging, against the wall.

A voice said dustily behind my shoulder, "Expect you better come with me."

II

For the lengthiest part of this drawn-out silence I did nothing but stand there and wonder what sort of trap I had been shoehorned into. The situation was too pat, too fortuitous it appeared to me, to have been the un-aided result of coincidence.

Narrowly watching the fellow I'd struck push him-self off the wall, pull the fit of his coat more elegantly about him with eyes that declared this would not be forgotten, I cursed myself for seven kinds of a fool. The dusty voice back of me said with thin patience: "You can come along on your own two feet or be packed on a shutter. Which will it be, bucko?"

I looked at the saucer-round eyes of the woman and blew out my breath with a disgusted shrug. "All right."

"Unbuckle that gun rig and step out of it—careful."

When I had done so, the man back of me said, "You aim to prefer charges, Frelton?"

The fellow I'd struck had himself in hand now, though he still hadn't collected all the wind I'd spilled out of him. In a tone gruff with outrage he grumbled, "No charges."

The silence built up full of locked-away notions while the fat cook stared from behind his counter and the woman's glance nervously dropped from my face. The man back of me said, "Then perhaps you'll be good enough to pick up that shell belt."

Frelton grudgingly picked up the gun-weighted rig,

put it into the hand that reached round my left side and backed off, palely venomous, to right the kicked-over chair.

"You can turn around now," the fellow back of me said.

He was a tall stocky jigger with a brush of red bristles weighting down his upper lip, and his frame squeezed into a wrinkled suit of town duds whose open short-skirted coat showed a glint of polished metal where the lamps' light struck across it. And, as I'd more than half suspected, there was a pistol in his fist.

He tipped me a nod. "Let's go."

I put four bits beside my plate and, walking between tables, pushed through the door. The night seemed twice as black outside and damply smelled of the stagnant pools in that trash littered bed of Sycamore Creek.

"Well, where do we go from here?" I said when the law-giver packing my belt stopped beside me.

"Straight up the street."

The gun he had held was back in its holster but I did not think this augured too much. He had a look of hard competence. I said, "Isn't this just a little high-handed, Marshal? What happens if I decide not to play?"

"Your privilege, McGrath."

We looked at each other. I cursed under my breath. I could see him pretty good by now and did not care for the sight of his teeth behind that twisted steel-trap grin. If he had me pegged—as he obviously did—there was a deal more behind this than being locked up for disturbing the peace. "Am I under arrest?"

"I would say, offhand, that depends on you. Why don't you just string along for a spell and see what develops? That way, mebbe, there won't be nobody hurt."

"Mind saying where you're taking me?"

"You might say we're going to see a man about a dog. Now," he said, drawling, "if it's all right with you, perhaps we'd better get going."

I had a feeling deep inside I wasn't going to like this. When you start getting double talk from his kind of jasper it's a lead pipe cinch you're playing for more than table stakes. I considered this, scowling, unable to come up with any handy way around it. Like he'd said, if I wanted to play along, I might reasonably expect to get there in one piece. If I balked, I was going to have a fight on my hands and I'd likely wind up in the same place anyway.

I struck out up the street without further gab but the shadows we went through weren't dark as my thoughts. If he'd got hold of my name, he had to know considerable more.

It looked a pretty sure bet I was the dog he had mentioned, and there was nothing in that notion to reassure a man who'd run up the debts that I had. The law called them debts to society. But there was more to those capers than had been worked out.

In my head I went over this grab again. He'd either known where to come or that shot had pulled him into the place, and it was dollars to doughnuts he had known where I was from the minute I left my horse at that livery. This taffy-haired dame hadn't sucked me into it whether she was Frelton's wife or something else. Pete McGrath had a heap too much on his mind to be taking time out to play at squire with a woman. I'd gone in there looking for a hound to kick and Frelton had obliged by acting like one.

Fiddle squeal was coming from a big lighted place that looked like a deadfall on this side of the street some thirty yards ahead. Twenty feet short of this, the marshal put out a hand. "Cut across toward the store and stay out of that light."

I cut over to the store with him practically on my heels and stopped by the steps that climbed to its porch. For a star packer this marshal showed some oddly puzzling habits. Once more his arm came out to stop me. While we stood there silent he took a long look around. He jerked his chin out ahead. "Keep on like you're goin' till you reach that vacant lot."

When we got there he did some more looking round. "We'll cut back over to the other side now—"

"Don't you know where you hang your hat, mister?"

"We're not going to my office. Not straight off anyway."

I swung back across, keeping out of the lights, wondering what the hell he was up to. The idea began to grow in my mind that this redheaded marshal for some damn reason wasn't hugging the notion of being seen in my company. "I ain't got nothing that's catching," I told him.

All the answer I got to that you could hear with both ears shut. With the flat of a hand he pushed me on. I couldn't think what was ailing him. For all I could see, we had the street to ourselves; there was no traffic certainly, two-legged or otherwise. It didn't make sense a marshal antigodlin around in this fashion.

Pressing closer he said, mouth near enough to let me feel the scrape of his bristles: "That next buildin', McGrath. Turn left just beyond it. When you reach the backside of it, bear left again."

I slanched a dark look at him. "Mind telling me what all this pussyfooting's for?"

"We got a mort of nosy bastards hangin' round this burg right now."

"And you're thinking someone might spring me—is that what's fretting you?"

"Get movin'," he grumbled, "an' save the rest of that wind to blow on your porridge."

I felt like a fool, slipping round that corner like a ten year old toting off somebody's melon. It crossed my mind I might turn out to be one, time we got to wherever this tinbadge was taking me. With him staying just out of grabbing range, I cut left as directed, then left once again and stopped as, cat wary, he came up alongside.

"Up them stairs an' don't try nothin' fancy."

In the room at the top of the stairs, when we entered, a man in his fifties with a bulge of an abbot sat hunched over a desk that was scruffy with papers. His glance flicked up briefly, skewering me, searching, as the red-headed lawman pushed the door to behind us. "Lock it," he grunted, returning his look to the map spread before him, marking something with a pen which he laid aside then.

"Major, this here's the feller I was tellin' you about—Pete McGrath," the marshal said, with his back against the door.

The shirtsleeved fat man picked up a pipe, peered at me again and knocked out the dottle against the flat of a hand. A pair of eyes that was two shades bluer than a well chain scraped my length with the feel of a currycomb and stayed anchored on me while he repacked the briar from a pouch of Lone Jack.

"He don't look so much," the fat man said.

Against the door in back of me, the badge packer chuckled while the heat boiled up around the bind of my wipe. "Well, he ain't much for bark an' that's a fact, but when it comes down to bite, you might talk to Fingers Frelton."

"What's Frelton got to do with the tax on apples?"

"I dunno about apples but, when it comes to hog-legs, McGrath just shot his out of Frelton's paw and spread him flat against a wall for good measure."

The potbellied jasper behind the desk, still considering me with that wintry stare, scraped a match to life and diddled the flame across the bowl of his pipe. When he got the thing going, he dropped the match in a saucer and said through a cloud of blue smoke: "What was all that about?"

"They was over to Chow Ming's. Frelton was there with Angie, feeding his tapeworm, when McGrath here dropped in. Frelton didn't like something said by his woman an' fetched her a cuff. McGrath called him on it."

I said, "Who's this Frelton that you make such a squawk about?"

"Barkeep at the Buffalo Bull—deals a little faro between the whisky sours," the fat man said, pushing his words through the smoke. "Frelton doesn't matter—it's you we're here to talk about."

"Why me, and who's *we?*"

He said around the pipe, "I'm sorry. Marshal there's Red Durphey. I'm Gil Shannon—that mean anything to you?"

It didn't straightoff, yet there was something about it. . . . I took another hard look at that nearly bald noggin and the scraggle of head hair curling round his collar, and suddenly it came to me. *Major* Gil Shannon. Of course! He'd been practically a household name across three-quarters of this spread-out country—Giff Pinchot's pet troubleshooter, newly appointed supervisor if the proposed Tonto National Forest ever became an established fact.

But I still couldn't get hold of what that had to do with me, and said so.

The major was a man who could be equally blunt. "It's a long, devious story. There's been a lot of opposition to the President's proposals, though you can see all around you the need for such a project. Oddly enough, those who need this most are among its bitterest enemies—it's hard to see how folks can be so goddam stupid," he said with an irritated edge to his voice. "If the timber isn't protected, this whole watershed will go. But they don't want regulations, they want the Tonto left alone. They like things just the way they are around here, in control of the boys who can hire the most guns. They don't give a tinker's dam about the country, or what exploitation and their interminable feuds can do it if this greed isn't curbed."

I pushed it around while I studied his face, the bulge of broad shoulders, that pale blue stare, the scarred fist round his pipe, the aggressive jaw that solidly held within it the grip of that steel-trap mouth. "So what's all of that to me?" I growled.

"A chance," he said, skreaking back in his chair. "A chance to do something for your country—"

"My country's Texas," I said with curled lip.

"Texas is part of the West—"

"Texas is the country that put a price on my scalp. As you damn well know! You must be scraping the bottom of the barrel if you've got down to me."

He pushed the tobacco deeper into his pipe with a stubby finger and touched another match to it. He said through the smoke, "I was hoping you would see this as a chance to set the record straight."

"Is that what you're offering?"

"I'm offering you a choice, McGrath. You're headed for a noose, if some excited posseman don't gun you out of the saddle first."

"That might take some doing," I said.

"Sooner or later that's how you'll end up. As things stand right now, you can measure your life expectancy in terms not of months, not of weeks but in days, maybe hours. They've got your likeness plastered over four states. Perhaps you've given them the slip for the moment but once those dodgers catch up with you, you've had it.

"You killed your first man in San Saba—a banker. You were caught, stood trial for it, convicted and, because you refused to testify, were sentenced to life imprisonment. You caused quite a sensation by keeping your mouth shut.

"You were brought up right I seem to remember, had been ranching someplace around Iowa Park when you rode into San Saba and shot that fellow. The law couldn't find any connection between you: the 'mystery killer' the newspapers called you.

"After serving two years, you managed to escape. Three months later you killed a sheriff in Galveston and got clean away. Twenty-eight days ago you were seen looking up stage schedules at Pecos, but again got clear after wounding a marshal. You think that kind of luck will hold up?"

"I'll take my chances."

"Think again," Shannon said, putting down his pipe. "The law's not as stupid as you appear to imagine—incompetent sometimes, but with a very long arm. I've been just about certain you were going to show up here."

He sat quiet for a bit, giving me time to digest this. It didn't make sense that a man in his job should have kept tabs on me. Or been able to, even. I must have showed my distrust. Nodding, he said, "I looked for a pattern, plotted your course and came up with an answer. Does the name 'Gold Spur Charlie' surprise you?"

He could see that it did. It surprised the hell out of me. I pulled my jaws back together.

"I've been to a lot of trouble to get hold of you, McGrath."

There was a taste in my mouth. I got the message

all right. He'd said I had a choice. "I cooperate or get sent back under guard to stand trial for what happened to that Galveston sheriff."

"That's about the size of it," Red Durphey said back of me.

When Shannon's look went doorward past me, I blew out my breath in a disgusted snort. "What kind of a chore have you roped out for me?"

The major said, "How much do you know about that Four Peaks country?"

"You mean this side of the Apache Trail?" When he nodded I told him, "All I know about that you could put in your eye and no one, by God, would ever know it was there."

"All the better." He smiled. "I can't afford to send a man with preconceived notions or one sufficiently familiar with the terrain and situation that he'd take anything for granted. I want a man who'll keep his shoulder to the wheel, keep both eyes peeled and be tough enough not to get pushed around, bought off or caught in a bind because he can't or won't shoot."

We considered each other for a couple of heartbeats while I let what he'd said percolate through my thinking. "What happens if I run out on you?"

Flat as the prairie miles he said, "I don't expect you to be that foolish. What I'm asking you to do is dangerous—undercover. No credit and no glory, and if you get into trouble don't look this way because the Forest Service won't ever have heard of you. You'll be strictly on your own, without any kind of backing."

He pulled open a drawer, dug around inside, and tossed a roll of greenbacked currency which I caught lefthanded as he said in that cool half contemptuous voice: "This you can use for expenses; I don't care what you do with it. There won't be any more, and when you go through that door don't come back. Is that clear?"

"You don't want no report."

Shannon nodded. "What I want is results. I'll know either way."

"What about Durphey here?"

"He's got his own job to do." The major picked up his pipe, whipped another match to flame. Waved the smoke away from that hardbitten face. "Pressure's being put where it will be the most felt. Congressional seats will be up for grabs in a couple of months. Most of those presently warming them would sleep a lot sounder if they had some assurance they'd be getting them back. These are the people who are being most worked on.

"Here in Arizona—in New Mexico, too—a number of interests usually antagonistic have lately got together to try and put a stop to the creation of further Forest Reserves. This combine has got power and a considerable amount of good hard cash; it's made up of sheepmen, some of the cattle associations, and various vested lumber interests. It's not hard to see what has brought this about. To the stockmen, these Reserves represent a lot of changes when considered in the light of present range practices. It's being claimed National Forests will spell the end of the open range—neither sheep nor cattle are going to stand still for that. Restrictions of any sort are anathema to these agrarian despots who thrive on the conditions they've themselves set up—where might is all that's needed to insure fat profits from use of public lands."

"Kind of depends, don't you think?"

Shannon's stare took on a wintry glint. "Teddy Roosevelt doesn't think so. He understands what private enterprise—let go unchecked—will do to this country. Maybe you'll find it hard to believe, but a few years ago the Santa Cruz valley from Tucson to Nogales was grassed stirrup deep and filled with black walnuts. People have been cutting down those trees for firewood. In less than ten years, if the stockmen around there continue to fetch in more and more cattle, they're going to have nothing but sixty miles of desert.

"It's to stop such wholesale wanton destruction that the President's pushing to get more Reserves. These National Forests won't ruin the big ranchers—they can buy more range if they're running more stock than we can give them permits for, but these reserves will save the small independents with limited capital. And there's the water situation, the need to protect timber—"

"Just what is it you want *me* to do?"

"I want the pressure taken off those boys back in Washington. I want you to break up this unholy alliance."

III

"Your gall should take you far," I said, but that cold, shallow stare looked back unblinking.

"When you've run through all the appropriate words, you've still got to face the unpleasant fact you and I have in common at the moment. Two white chips in a no-limit game. Expendable, both of us.

"I happen to believe Teddy Roosevelt's right, but that doesn't take Pinchot off my back. And as long as he's breathing down my neck, you're going to find me like a rope around yours."

I'm not a man to be easily impressed but I could see he meant every word he said. It was in that stare, in the tone of his voice. The whole Forest movement was caught in a bind—I'd heard a few rumbles about that myself, and the President wasn't one to take a licking without putting up one hell of a scrap.

So what it boiled down to, apparently, was me. A

man who had been too free with his gun. There just wasn't any way to talk myself out of this.

Locust sound in the night outside began to rasp through my thinking, like the throb of a tooth. It came over me suddenly how still the room had got with myself staked out between two pairs of eyes like a fool hen trapped in a finger drawn circle. What the hell was I waiting on?

"You've made your point," I told Shannon grimly. "It's plain what you want, how far you'll go to get it. What else should I know?"

"This bunch isn't satisfied with blocking proposed extension of Reserves already established—their lame ducks at the Capitol have been instructed to filibuster all proposed changes to present grazing laws. The Chief Forester is convinced that sheep are destructive to grass and has been trying mighty hard to get them barred from the Forests. As things stand right now, this is one of the changes that'll probably get shelved.

"The combine, meanwhile, is working tooth and toenail to get more territory set aside for use of the sheep crowd. Easiest way is to show previous use. They're planning, we think, to make a start in this area, pushing sheep onto ground currently held by cattle; if they can take this over, they've established usage—"

"If this outfit's as one-minded and all-seeing as—"

"It's pretty solid at the moment," the major said, smiling thinly, "but I don't think the lower echelons, on the cow side anyway, have got wind yet of the upper crust's strategy. The long drought we've had and consequent gutted condition of the market have just about driven small owners to the wall. The cattle barons in the policy making top segment of this combine couldn't care less what happens to the raggedy-ass contingent whom they tend to consider little better

than rustlers. They'd be glad to have these boys put
out of business."

"You got any notion who's picked to move in on
them?"

Something changed in his stare or it may have been
the way that pipe put smoke around him. "The ones
in the know have been pretty cagey." He said, sounding thoughtful, "I can't honestly say. But I *think*—basing
this on things I've been told about methods he's used
elsewhere—it'll probably be Rabas."

Something sharp turned over and coldly stirred in
my guts.

Shannon said: "Those who've had the courage to take
a stand and fight back have pretty generally taken a
beating they couldn't manage to survive. They've been
shot, jailed and lynched. This feller sends out his scouts
and when they've hit on a place that for one reason or
another appears at all vulnerable he moves in with
hard cash and buys off the law. Then he brings in his
sheep—ninety, a hundred thousand of the critters—
and nothing stands before him."

Yeah. I knew a little something about this Rabas from
experience. His trail and mine had crossed when Gold
Spur Charlie had been gun boss of the Yaquis Rabas
hired to put his blattin woolies across cowmen's deadlines. A man who runs cattle can get pretty knuckle-
headed. Most of them hold a preconceived notion that
a man who herds sheep is just as stupid as his charges.

I had never met Rabas but, from what I'd uncovered
of Charlie's methods, I had a pretty vivid picture of
the sort of jigger this sheep king was. *Feed my sheep*
was all the instructions his herders got. He fetched
most of his help from below the Line, big pushed-
around Yaquis so hopped up on peyote they stood
ready to kill at the drop of a hat. Armed with .30-30s
and the prospect of eating all the beef they could hold,

Rabas' army of fighting sheepmen had become an ugly, hard-hitting fact. They weren't much for pretty but they rolled across the range flattening everything before them, and if this were your intention they certainly got the job done.

"Marshal, here, mentioned the town being filled with nosy galoots. Anything there I should know about?"

"Well, that feller you just tangled with, Frelton, hangs around more or less with a pretty rough crowd; I've an idea he's repping for the lumber interests. We've not managed, so far, to uncover any local rep for the railroads—I doubt they're involved very deeply. The cow crowd, locally, doesn't know what's going on yet and probably won't till Rabas hits them."

"No big spreads around here or Four Peaks?"

"None you'd consider in the cattle baron class. Only one even comes close—Rocking Arrow. Kay Wilbur. Seems to have weathered this drought better than most." He looked into his pipe and fired up again.

"It's pretty much up to you how you handle this business. I'd like these small spreads protected if you can find a way to do it and I'd be a lot happier—a lot easier in my mind—if there were less of this riffraff shacked up around here. Your main job, however, is to stir up dissension in the ranks of this goddam alliance. If we can get them squabbling among themselves, get some of that heat taken off those politicians in Washington—"

He broke off to stare at my uplifted hand.

I had thought to hear the skreak of a stair tread and twisted my head to throw a look at the door. Durphey, backing away from it, tossed the rolled rig he had confiscated. Flipping it round me, I palmed my artillery just as the door was flung violently open.

Three broadfaced galoots spilled into the room in a

glint of held weapons, a fourth vaguely showing at the top of the stairs.

Sheep smell was lost in the acrid stench of flame wreathed pistols. In this deafening clamor, smoke swirled and jumped. The lamp went out in those pounding explosions. The recoil of that bucking Colt in my fist was the first good feeling I had known in hours. The screams of the dying didn't bother me a bit.

As suddenly as it had started, the jamboree was over. With the jarred air still pulsing from the rumbling echoes, the major struck a match behind me, struck another and got the lamp lit.

Just inside the half wrecked door, two crumpled shapes of dead meat lay. Across the sill, with sweat damp hair plastered round his chin, was another, eyes rolled into the back of his skull. Down the stairs' dark planks was a trail of blood.

"You'll do," Shannon said.

IV

Drought and sun and furnace driven winds had given this Four Peaks country the nightmare look of a blasted range. From the beds of long-dry washes, sparse clumps of yellowed galleta grass showed, a mockery to the listless skin and bones cattle seen standing stiff legged, too far gone even to twitch at flies. Buzzards planed through the glare of sky; others glimpsed on the ground were staggering around, too bloated to flap away at my approach—and the stink was enough to make a man puke.

Bones were strewn about the cracked surface of each infrequent waterhole encountered. Several times, in the distance, I'd sighted dismounted cowhands swinging

axes in this killing heat. busting up cactus, cutting down
the green barked wood of tiny-leafed paloverdes while
drearily ringed by walleyed cattle, too stiff in the joints
of their thorn burred legs to do anything but mournfully
low.

A man unused to traveling cow country might with
reason have wondered if Rabas was insane to covet
a range as desolate as this. No dude, of course, could
be expected to know what a good soaking rain would
do for this country—not that any such blessing appeared at all imminent. The overhead brightness was
like a brass bowl, holding trapped heat hard against
the blistered earth.

Though I'd not gone out of my way, quitting Sunflower, to keep my departure secret, I had not noticed
any great amount of interest being displayed in my com-
ings and goings throughout the two extra days I'd
elected to stay there. To have left straight off on the
heels of that fracas in Shannon's office would have
been pretty stupid; still, I could very well have become a marked man after shouting the major off the
street when those four had first figured to clean his
plow.

So I wasn't unmindful that I might not be as alone as
it looked. I couldn't detect any signs of surveillance
but that hombre who'd left his blood on the stairs had
not been found, so it rather looked like he'd got back
with his story to whoever had set up those attempts
to take Shannon out of this play. They might not yet
have put a name to me but it wasn't much likely they'd
be careless enough not to figure me into their working
agenda.

The morning grew hotter as the day advanced. I
didn't like the way I'd been dragged into this, hauled
by my bootstraps up out of the bog of uncaring futility
I had been plunged into by that news about Charlie.

It was right what they said about God and His wonders, if He was responsible for cheating me out of an intention I'd nursed and put each waking thought to ever since getting clear of that damned prison farm. If ever a man needed killing, it was Charlie. But the way of his going—taken off in some senseless two-bit saloon brawl—made a gut twisting mockery of everything I had stood for.

Along about ten, or it may have been later, while skirting the rim of a deepening canyon, toilfully climbing into the uplands where the lifted hot winds off the desert turned gusty and pungent with the smell of scorched ground, I chanced to look down. And saw, a hundred feet lower in the bed of that boulder-strewn, grassless gorge, an off-his-horse rider industriously chopping at a giant saguaro, a pair of listless cow brutes indifferently watching.

The great thorny cactus toppled, bursting wide on the rock hot ground. The cows staggered nearer and dropped heads between spraddled bony legs as they endeavored to munch the bitter thorn-guarded pulp. Melon smell and the pungence of turnip came spinning up on a gyrating dust devil.

Wiping the sweat from gritty cheeks, I kneed my tired gelding on. In the last two hours I'd counted four dozen carcasses; all that was keeping these cow spreads alive was such gruelling labor as that I'd just watched, chores no self-respecting hand would ordinarily perform. Not a solitary calf, alive or dead, had I seen. If the sheepmen came, as Shannon foretold, it would mean the end for most of these outfits.

Slant of sun dripped like molten copper, throwing its fiery gleam across the land. The hush of desolation was all about like the dust this wind uncaringly scattered over every living thing. I peered about through red-

rimmed eyes and cursed each gulch and rock-ribbed
peak.

If it had not been for sheep in the first place, these
boys wouldn't be out chopping cactus. There'd have
been enough graze on these upper ranges to have carried their dying critters through.

You'd have guessed at first sight Bad News was a
ghost town, for if ever a community looked the part,
the false-fronted shacks I came suddenly onto in the
wind-rippled bend of a gloomy gulch had all the earmarks. Even rude frames whipsawed from a roundabout stand of pines told the whole story of blasted
hopes.

Weathered to a drab and uniform gray, these appeared as empty as the wind-ridged dust of the trail
itself, too cramped even here to be called a street. The
half obliterated legends seemed more the boast of times
long gone than with any foundation in current fact.
There was one hotel, a great barn of a saloon, a store
of sorts and one sagging stable with an appended shed
roof built over the dead smell of a fireless forge. All
else was a let go hodgepodge of gaping windows and
weeds and cactus standing tall through the splintery
planks of roofless remains that might once have been
porches.

This was more than I'd glimpsed in that first rang-
ing glance, for dusk lay deep in near-black shadows
with never a telltale spark of light throughout the whole
length of this gash in the hills. But men were here and
I presently observed two in the half caught flutter of
tiny adjustments. A seated gent rose and soundlessly
moved from his place in the murk of the hotel's veranda, silently fading through the open front door. By
the blacksmith's forge someone else cuffed a hat above
sharpened stare and eased one spread-fingered fist to-

ward a hip. Night air pulsed a coolness down this
track and touched the short hairs at the back of my
neck without moving anything else in sight.

I swung the gelding's head toward the stable, and
the fellow I had glimpsed by the forge sauntered over
and gave me a stiffly searching look. After which, without opening his mouth, he spun round and took off,
gone, no doubt, to get the word passed around.

In the course of those months I had spent hunting
Charlie, this had become pretty near an unfailing ritual
in the towns I'd been through. Most noticeable perhaps
in such hideyholes as this, the smaller, the forgotten,
the tucked-away places. Like a stone chunked into an
open-topped well, the ripples went out. An off-his-beat
drummer, a fugitive trying to drop out of sight, could
sometimes cause more excitement than a gent riding in
with a star on his vest. I suppose this was understand-
able. They didn't have to ask what a badge had flashed
its shine for.

I swung down before the open maw of the stable.
An old codger presently shuffled out to take the reins
—a lean, hard-twisted leather faced jigger. With them
looped over an arm, he lit the lantern he was carrying
and hung its bale from a hook above the entrance. This
dodge, too, I'd encountered before; it was done to give
him a close-up look at me.

He was a cooler hand than that forgeside idler, his
glance barely brushing the side of my face before he
was bending to pick up a hoof, pretending engross-
ment to cover the mumble of words let drop from the
side of his mouth. "Don't you ever give up?"

I was shaping a smoke from my sack of Duke's Mix-
ture when the man's muttered query came. I didn't
look round until the old duffer straightened and then
could not place him; not too surprising considering the
numbers of faces I'd peered at. But it was plain he

remembered me. The immediate question was what to do about it.

I still hadn't reached a satisfactory conclusion when— not waiting for an answer—he strode away with my horse. There wasn't a heap I could do if he wanted to tie his bit to the fact of my arrival. A threat most likely would only put his back up and bribes, I had noticed, seldom guaranteed anything.

It seemed, staring after him, I'd precious little choice. If I was to serve Shannon's purpose there was nothing could help me better than fear. And the only fear likely to move this deal forward was the kind a man gets staring into a gun.

What the Forest Bill needed right now was a distraction, something which might hopefully set this jumble of unlikely bedfellows at each other's throats, keep them worked up to where they'd time for nothing else.

A pretty tall order.

I was mightily tempted to haul my freight. But what else could I find to fill up the hole Charlie's death had left in an interminable stretch of empty tomorrows? A risk would help, and there was plenty of it here. There wasn't a chance of concealing my identity if this jasper decided to flap his lip. His knowledge committed me as nothing else could have. I struck out for the hotel, the gun riding heavy on my hip as I walked.

Where the deadfall's lit lamps cut bright shafts through the deepening dark, spilling butter yellow light across a line of racked horses that hadn't before been there, I saw a knot of booted hombres gathered about the jigger who'd been idling by the forge.

As I came nearer, heralded by the ching of spur rowels, the group suddenly shifted, opening up a little, so that I caught a good look at the one who'd quit the smithy. He was still on the fringe, all its interest apparently taken up with two others, the light shining full on the chin-strapped face of a burly shape in bullhide chaps. This was the one who had their attention and he looked of a mind to make the most of it.

He had a loud, taunting voice. The gent he was baiting, though his back was toward me, looked frail by comparison—some greenly awkward kid, I thought, and pushed into the group, shoving men off my elbows.

The bully's victim turned out to be a girl. The big talker, intent on his fun and obviously pleased by the attention he was getting, scarcely gave me a glance. I caught sheep smell again as the fellow flung an arm out to snap callused fingers in the face of the girl. "You haven't got a waddy on your whole damn payroll with half enough guts to—"

I said, breaking in, "You prepared to bet on that?"

V

His head came round like he couldn't believe it. This was one too used to getting his own way and the build-up from this stared out at me now with the amused sort of insolence that came of suspecting a new source of sport.

Crossed belts supported a gun at either hip. His black sombrero had been made below the border. Dark bull-hide chaps were tricked out with silver conchas. He had coarse black hair above a swarthy jaw and a high-boned look that suggested some of his forebears might have been more at home in moccasins than pants. "You always pick on women?" I asked.

His derisive stare went over me again. With a wink for his audience and a hand cupped back of an ear he said, "You'll have to speak up—"

"This loud enough for you?" I inquired and, leaning

into it, delivered four knuckles hard against his chin. The cocksure face went snapping back, the folding chest went rocking with it and he was suddenly flat on his back in the lamp-yellowed dust.

A man never knows when he bites into one, which way a goddam pickle will squirt, and not all of your bullies pack two guns for bluff. Watching this fellow, I saw raging fury replace his astonishment. He came twisting around like a broken-backed crab, breathing hard, the shine of his eyes malevolently hunting.

He shoved onto an elbow, got a knee beneath him to slam a hand streaking hipward. You could hear the sound of steel torn from leather. There was a bright gout of flame as gun thunder clouted and bounced off the building fronts.

I was not where the bullet went. Before he could get off another shot, my boot sent the pistol skittering out of his grip.

"You fool!" I said. "I ought to bend that hogleg across your noggin!"

He shoved to his feet. A parched twist of grin pulled the lips off his teeth. The eyes above blanched cheeks were ugly. "You got a handle?" he rasped through half strangled frustration.

"McGrath . . . Pete McGrath."

It was plain the name meant nothing to him. I watched his look go from me to the girl and come back, bitter, narrowing, darkly filled with speculation. He backed up, bent, and retrieved his pistol, cuffing it against a palm to get the dust out. He hesitated, pulled two ways, but caution won.

Putting the best face he could on this, he dropped the belt gun into its sheath and stood, meanly smiling, running his dark stare over my face.

"I reckon you're the Rockin' Arrow ramrod—the *new*

one," he sneered. "It's nothin' to get so proud about. She hires 'em regular once a month an'—"

"Does she?" I said with a quick step toward him.

Temper burned like a fire in his brain and the slant of those cheeks grew purely wicked. I expect my own lent no balm to weak hearts. He backed off a step. The sneer fell away. A kind of pale fright peered out of bulged eyes and the cramped legs kept moving, back pedaling till a groping hand found the horse behind him.

I saw it catch at the horn, close round it convulsively. He seemed anchored there, uncertain and shaken, unable to tear his eyes from my face.

"No . . ." he gasped in a voice filled with curds. "No!" he growled, pushing a hand out between us and trying to pull himself together. Some of the fright began to leach from his stare. He said too loud in a blustery voice, "This range ain't goin' to be big enough for both of us. You better git while you're able because next time our tracks cross—"

"Don't waste no dinero on that bet," I told him. "You've had your lesson. Now I'll give you plain warning: never let me find you on Rocking Arrow land."

I wheeled away, disregarding his apoplectic look. To the girl I said, "Let's get whacking. If your visiting's done, it's time we were lining out for headquarters."

I wasn't too sure we could carry this off, leastways without gunplay. But I chucked one cool look quickly around, noting its visible effect on those nearest, feeling the girl's hand tighten on my arm.

From his seat in the saddle the big jasper called: "I'll be remembering you."

"I'd be some put out," I grunted, "if you didn't."

It was the girl, this belted boss of Rocking Arrow, that finally broke our riding silence. "You've made a bad enemy," she said, shaking her head. "Telesco won't be forgetting that, mister." Her eyes searched the look of my straight ahead face and the sigh seemed brought up from the bottom of her lungs. "It's been said he can nurse humiliations like an Apache."

I could feel the look of her still going over me and could easily imagine the pile of things she hadn't asked. Apparently she subscribed to the West's old-fashioned notion that a man be taken on current behavior and his past left untouched wherever he had buried it. By and large, I considered this an admirable philosophy.

She sighed again. "There are times when even the sincerest of thanks is bound to sound trifling. But I am very grateful," she said, with a huskiness suggesting inner turmoil. "This isn't the first time that fellow's bothered me."

"What's he do for a living, besides pester women?"

"I would guess 'pistolero' pretty well sums him up."

"He smells like a sheepman."

I felt the jump of her eyes. "That's from being around Rabas. They went through here last year on their way to Pleasant Valley. . . . They could have found a closer way."

"Yeah. I heard about that. He's probably come back to look up old friends. Rocking Arrow have anything to do with those deadlines?"

"My father and his range boss were killed trying to hold them."

It figured. According to Shannon, Rocking Arrow was the biggest outfit this side of the Basin and it was top priority in Rabas' strategy to hit where his strike would make the greatest impression, object lessons being part of his credo. The Toms, Dicks and Harrys of the cattle fraternity were pretty easily managed once the local moguls had been taken care of.

"How long has this feller been around these parts?"

"Long enough to lay pipe. He came in during calf roundup. He bought out Hy Ferguson—the Boxed O north of us."

I pushed it around, picking up loose ends. A petticoat spread, an outfit run by a woman, usually found it pretty rough to keep hands, particularly ramrods. Not too many capable men in this kind of business cared to work for a woman and, with a prod like Telesco hanging round to lean on them, it took no great flight of imagination to get to the bottom of her trouble. She didn't look the kind that would willingly knuckle under. But running a ranch was a man's sort of business. With her controls scared away no woman was going to stand very long against Rabas.

"What's Telesco doing with this Ferguson place?"

"I haven't been over there."

"You must have heard a few things."

"Nothing definite," she said. "He doesn't encourage visiting."

"What's he done with the cattle?"

She looked at me sharply, presently shrugging. "That's what Mahoney, my last foreman, asked. He had our boys poking round till a couple of them were shot at."

"Then he quit?"

"That's right," she said grimly. "Him and both hands —the pair that were shot at."

"How many men has Telesco got over there?"

"We don't know that, either." She considered me out of the corners of her glance. "You let him think you'd taken Mahoney's place. Any chance of your being induced to do that?"

It would certainly give me a reason for being here. "Not sure," I said, "I could work for a woman. Pretty set in my ways . . . might turn out they're not your ways. For me to do you any good, I'd have to have a free hand—"

"You've got it. There's one thing, though," she told me, looking worried, "I suppose you'd better understand straight off. The job pays sixty a month. If things keep on like they've been these past months, you might have to take it in cows or paper."

"That's a bridge we won't have to cross till we get there."

We rode without speech for half a mile or so. I didn't much care whether she took me on or not. It might help in the job I'd been sent here to do, if I made up my mind to go through with it, which I hadn't.

Sure, I'd come this far. Because it suited me to do so. I had been at loose ends when that hard-faced Shannon had put me in a corner. Making out to be convinced had looked the quickest way to be free of him and that marshal's tin they had hung on Durphey. I didn't doubt they could send me back to the rockpile, but where I was now they would first have to catch me. If I decided to run, I had a pretty good start.

"You're no chuck-line rider," the girl said abruptly. "How did you happen to be in this country?" She looked at me slanchways. "You packing some kind of tin?"

That was a laugh if a man had the mood for it. "No tin," I said, and put up both hands. "You may look if you'd like."

She flushed but said cool enough, "I don't think that will be necessary," and let me see by the cut of her eyes she had no intention of becoming that personal. Like as if I gave a damn!

VI

Summer's smell and creosote stink lay strong in the wind whipped off the desert, and a late moon dropped its silver haze across purpled slopes of distant hills. I said, "Just how rough's this drought been on you?"

"It hasn't been just . . . well, bad enough. Ranch is still mine, but that's more the result of Father's foresight than owing to anything I've managed to do. Market's never been nearer the bottom and if more cows are dumped we may all be sold up. The four hands we've still got haven't been paid in six months—they haven't even drawn smoking in over seven weeks.

"I suppose," she said bleakly, "I've had it better than most. We haven't yet had to put a plaster on it. Most of the others have gone that route. Bank's already taken over three spreads—probably sitting up nights trying to figure what to do with them. I don't honestly think they would give me a loan."

I wished I could see her face a little plainer.

She said after a moment, "If the sheep come through here again this year you can have it for taxes."

"Stands to reason they will."

Her glance came round. "What gives you that notion?"

"Well . . ." I shrugged. "Take this Telesco. He doesn't look the kind that would have two nickels he could rub together. Yet you say he's bought in. You said he was through here last year with Rabas. Where you reckon he got the price for Boxed O?"

She thought about that. Said more firmly, "The place went for peanuts. He wouldn't need Rabas' money."

"I'm afraid, Miss Wilbur, you don't understand Rabas.

Think back a bit to those deadlines you mentioned. Your father and his foreman got killed in that fracas. The sheep went through. What was done about it?"

"Nothing," she said flatly, "but it's going to be different if he tries that again."

People, I reckoned, believed what they wanted to. I shook my head. "Across three states cowmen have been up against Rabas and his sheep. Texas, New Mexico and Arizona have all had a taste of him and everywhere you go folks say it'll be different if he tries that again. It will only be different if you and other owners will put aside your wishbones and learn to face facts. How do you suppose he gets away with these things?"

"Tell me."

"He doesn't go into this blind. He has no range of his own and never did have. Wherever possible he feeds his sheep on public domain, state and federal lands if they come handy; where they don't, those Yaqui camp movers just throw their gray blanket across whatever happens to get in the way. The ones put in charge of his various bands know without asking what Rabas would tell them. *Feed my sheep.* He doesn't care how they do it."

She said, sounding angry: "There are laws in this country—"

I swore under my breath with the old bitter thoughts. "You're plumb right about that. But laws get interpreted by those who enforce them; laws, Miss Wilbur, in the final analysis turn out to be people, and people can be bought. Rabas has made a real art of the business!"

I didn't wait for her protest. I'd been over everything she could possibly say. "In the long haul," I told her, "his way's a lot cheaper than trying to raise sheep on land bought and paid for."

She thought about that, the shape of her stiffening as she peered at my face. "There are bound," she said resentfully, "to be a few rotten apples, but people don't always elect crooks to public office!"

"Of course they don't. They try to pick men they believe will serve their interests. It's the office that makes crooks of them, the pressures, the temptations. Would you risk your life daily for the kind of wages most badge toters get? For the miserly backing us righteous folks give them?"

She didn't like that. "If you want these things changed," I said, "you've got to face up to them. We all like to have our cake and eat it, too. Where there's trouble in the wind, we don't like to get involved. We find it easier to sit back and decry the lack of justice. We can howl to high heaven but until we're willing to put our shoulders to the wheel, the Rabases of this world are going to keep right on reaping the fruits of our labor."

The weight of her stare seemed a heap less friendly than the appraisal I'd got at the start of this ride. "You seem to know," she said, "considerable about this sheep-man—"

"I'm not taking up for him."

"No. You sound more like a man with a grievance. Did Rabas run you out of the cow business, McGrath?"

"I wouldn't know that roughshod peckerneck from Adam!"

But I'd said it too quick. With too much growl in my voice. Knowing I couldn't leave it there, I grumbled, "We been over a lot of the same ground is all; he's had a heap of space in papers round and about. I'm just trying to put you in touch with the facts—"

"Facing up to the facts as you call it is what got my father killed by that outfit." She said with a natural resentment, "When they came through here last year there wasn't much browse left along the trails; we'd had a pretty dry summer—not like this but bad enough. Some of these smaller spreads were feeling the pinch. They wanted my father to take a stand against Rabas, said they'd back him.

"So a bunch of them and Dad, with the idea of talking them into going some other route, rode over to the sheep camp. Rabas was there himself with his sheep boss, Charlie Ostermann. They were willing to talk, even listened to our problems, nodding and agreeable as a couple of six-shooters in the same belt." she said bitterly. "And all the while this talk was going on, Rabas' herders were shoving the biggest part of those sheep deeper into the hills, gobbling up our best winter range!"

"And by the time you got wind of this, it was too late to stop them. They'd already ridden right over your deadlines. So your father and his foreman gathered up whoever was willing and headed hell-bent smack into an ambush." I said with a nod, "It's happened before. Then you found out there was no recourse in law. Where you folks jumped them wasn't patented land. They had, you were told, every right to protect their property."

When she finally spoke, she sounded real deep-down furious. "We should have stopped them, I guess, on our own land you mean."

"Might have helped but I doubt it. What you don't understand is that Rabas, before he ties into new country, sets up a deal with the law. He buys off the badge toters you elect to protect you. No"—I held up a hand—"he can't buy them all off; he's bound to run into a few that are hostile. When he runs into lawmen who won't play his game, he puts on a different show. Invites them out for a look at his sheep and lines up a handful of rifle packing Yaquis, lets 'em see how good those boys are with bullets. Maybe they cut down a tree or someone's prize bull. He don't have to threaten them in so many words. I've only heard of one who didn't get the message. Feller got killed in a stampede of cattle."

"What *can* we do?"

"Any of these folks around here packing irons?"

"They were all packing irons last year." She said, choked with feeling, "Fred Hurley killed a couple herders on Tonto Creek. The sheep crowd's lawyer got Fred the limit. They sent him to Yuma and finally hung him."

The skreak of leather, clink of shod hooves and the labored breath of our climbing horses were drops of sound in the night's shrouded stillness.

I could almost feel the whirl of her thoughts. She had pluck, all right—she wasn't about to admit herself whipped. Those stiffened shoulders didn't go with giving up.

"Haven't noticed many calves," I offered presently. When that didn't catch fire, "Too much drought, I suppose."

She shrugged without answering. Faced with ruin if the sheep came again, I was a little astonished they'd allowed Telesco to buy and settle here right in the midst of them. Cowmen weren't a forgiving breed. Some of them anyway had probably glimpsed already what the end would be and hoped by ignoring him to postpone that day.

I said, "I'll ride over and have a talk with him tomorrow."

Her head came around. "Have a talk with who?"

"This feller, Telesco."

"You want to get yourself killed?"

"He'll be cooled off by then. Might be I could put a flea in his bonnet." I pushed it around in my head for a while. "How many of your neighbors got a yen to sell out?"

"To a *sheep*man?"

"Their money will spend just as quick as any other."

"Are you pulling my leg?"

"Not really. Think about it. A lot of these outfits, from what you say, must be pretty hard hit."

She said finally, grudgingly, "Some of them, I suppose, would probably sell if cash were offered." She peered at me uncertainly. "He's already got a foothold. Why would he want to buy any more if you're so sure they're coming through here again? Why not just wait and let them drop in his lap?"

"Not him."

"I don't see much difference between him and Rabas."

"Better sharpen your eyes. There's a whole heap of difference. Size and guts, just to mention a couple. To get back to the meaningful part of this discussion, it wasn't those wool lovers I had in mind."

Seemed for a moment as though I had lost her, but there wasn't no dust in the wheels of her think box. Twisting around she half leaned from the saddle. Seen this close, the green eyes were narrowed to something partway between disbelief, hope and scorn. "No outside cowman would risk two cents—"

"If we could put the right combination together, I think I could get the money to swing it."

The scorn won out, liberally mixed with the temper that came from that fiery red hair. "All right," I said quietly, "would you look more kindly at a partnership deal?"

She had her mouth half opened. Abruptly she closed it, pulled in a fresh breath. "You and me?" she said finally.

"It would have to embrace more than just us two, a

combine of sorts. If we could get enough owners to throw in their outfits—"

"You don't know these people."

"Leave them out for the moment. For more range and mobility would *you* be willing to take on some partners?"

She didn't answer straight off. Presently, sighing, she said, "I don't know. The idea never occurred to me. I guess a lot would depend on how much say I might have and how big a share. Rocking Arrow, remember, is at least twice—"

"Straightaway, you wouldn't have *any* say."

Staring, unable to grasp such enormity, she burst out: "You're crazy! Who would be fool enough to throw his spread into that kind of deal? You must think we're all idiots!"

"It isn't what I think that matters. Your big problem now is those sheep and what to do about them. If they come as things stand there won't any of you have a piece of grass left to sit on."

We covered half a mile without further gab. Then, tentatively, she said, "Even if we agreed to such an outlandish proposal, I can't see we'd be any better off than we were last year when most of this crowd joined hands to get behind my father—"

"It's quite possible you wouldn't."

I could feel her eyes digging into me again. She made an untranslatable sound of annoyance. "If that's what you think we should do, convince me."

"There's a difference," I said, "between a loose working arrangement of independent owners and a profit sharing partnership with a single man calling the shots at the head of it. A man at whose word the whole push will jump."

"This bunch of two-bit Caesars you propose to amalgamate won't never agree on which of their number is fit—"

"That wouldn't come up. The Rocking Arrow Syndicate has already got its brass-collar dog." I watched those green eyes narrow in on me again. "First clause laid down in any workable arrangement will confirm the free hand you've already given him."

"Well!" she said on an outrush of breath. "When they passed around shyness it's a cinch you weren't at the head of the line."

"You won't get rid of these sheep by waving no handkerchief."

Her lips flattened out and then turned down at one corner. "Go ahead," I said. "You want to tell me now this bunch of knotheads you've got for neighbors will never stand still for passing me the reins."

"Why should they?" she demanded. "They don't know you from Adam's off ox."

"One or two of them might," I said, thinly grinning. "It won't take long to find out about that."

VII

I didn't next day drop by for that talk I'd suggested having with Rabas' man, the sneery-eyed Telesco. First thing we did after reaching the ranch was retire to her father's office to hash out the details of my proposed amalgamation.

She got out a map of the Four Peaks country and marked down for my benefit the location of all the roundabout outfits. The most of these apparently were one man operations. There were two exceptions, not counting Boxed O (Telesco's headquarters)—Lee Hardigan's Turtle, and the Gourd and Vine of Carlos Debarra. Debarra was nearest with four hands on his payroll. Hardigan, with three, was on the far side of Boxed O, directly in line with the way Rabas' sheep looked most likely to come.

"What about Hardigan? Think he'll go along with this?"

She turned away from the lamp to sink into the chair at the side of the desk. "He's kind of set in his ways," she said with a dryness not previously apparent, "but I expect he can be persuaded."

Her color seemed more florid as she leaned toward the map to put a finger on Gourd & Vine. "It's Debarra you'll have the most trouble with. He's one of those Spaniards of the old school—very proper, very polite, but a man who feels out of step with his environment. He's not been able to live up to what he has been fashioned to believe a Debarra's due. At one time his family owned this whole Basin clean on up to the Mogollon Rim."

"They pioneered this country?"

"They came in not too long after the Peraltas. It's been claimed his great-grandfather got it as a grant from the Spanish Crown. The courts ruled otherwise. He feels—not unnaturally—he's been made the victim of Yankee skulduggery. His present headquarters backs against Squaw Butte, some twelve thousand acres along Spring Creek—all he has left from the courts and gambling forebears."

"So he's apt to be touchy. All right, I'll remember."

"Tomorrow," she said, "I'll introduce you to the crew and you can ask these people over to hear your proposition. Right now, I'm beat. You can sleep tonight on the couch in the parlor."

I suppose I did some twisting and turning. I didn't sleep well or get to sleep soon, and it wasn't just the horsehair that kept jabbing into me. My mind kept picking over things she'd said and I had a few thoughts about the matters not mentioned during our various discussions. Like Gil Shannon and this National Forests business and the penchant cowmen had for taking patents on water while fattening their cattle on the public domain.

There wasn't, when you got right down to it, any great amount of difference between the business habits of either faction: both sought profit from the use of public lands. The cow crowd perhaps did a smidgen less damage than the sheep and timber pirates, but they were all tough nuts determined to wrest a fortune from the least amount of investment. You might say cowmen had more of a stabilizing influence.

Some outfit in Chicago had some years ago developed a fencing material—wire with barbs on it—which was getting quite popular in some parts of Texas; this was sold by the roll and dubbed by cowmen "the weedbender's friend." It was sure anathema to beef raisers but they were going, I reckoned, to have to get used to it. More and more farmers were fetching plows into this western country and, despite the upswing in violence, it looked like to a lot of folks we were about on the verge of the last of the open range.

There was a heap of crazy talk going around. Advocates of the status quo claimed the government was trying to strangle private initiative, furiously citing as cases in point the Homestead Act, the National Forests proposal and the growing demands for a National Parks system. That "posterity" talk was all razzle-dazzle designed to bilk fools who couldn't or wouldn't see beyond their own noses.

Regardless of how much truth there was to this, you couldn't tell a cowman—or sheepman for that matter—that "free grass" wasn't his inalienable right. Their whole economy was based on this assumption and they were bound to blow up over any restrictions which tended to narrow their fields of operations. It was openly said by some of these people that if the government kept on they would soon "have us all cooped up on reservations like a bunch of goddam Injuns!"

And here I was smack-dab in the middle. Sent to create a full scale distraction that, any way you eyed it, was like to get more blood spilled that a man could shake a stick at. What that hardcased major and his bosses deepdown wanted was a big enough ruckus to force those numbskulls back there in Washington to recognize the need of government controls. And nobody gave a damn how this was managed.

He had caught me just right, knocked all of a heap by the hole Charlie's passing had left in my itinerary. I might hate his guts for putting me in this kind of forked stick but, squirm as I might, almost anything was better than getting sent back to where I had come from, and the both of us knew it.

I found it hard to keep from admiring his shrewdness. The job plainly called for a gink without scruples and my own public record showed he'd locked both hands hard around the right lever. I'd been tried and found guilty, done just what I'd been charged with. He had every right to think with Charlie out of my way I was shaped to his purpose. I might tell myself he could go roll his hoop, but a lifetime in prison was a powerful deterrent when considered as the price of running out on him.

He had found me once; I'd no reason to think he couldn't do it again.

I hadn't bothered undressing beyond boots, hat and shell belt. I was up and had all three of them on when she knocked at the door to tell me breakfast was ready.

What sleep I had got hadn't done me much good and I expect I looked like hell warmed over when I stepped into that bright and cheery kitchen with its cloth-covered table laid for three and peered at the woman who stood by its side.

"I'd like you to meet my mother," Kay said, as she fetched a hot platter of ham and eggs from the hay-burner stove with its two spring cylinders. "Mother, shake hands with Pete McGrath, our new range boss."

Mrs. Wilbur looked thin with not much meat spread over her bones but she managed a smile as she took my hand to bid me welcome. You could see the resemblance in eyes and hair, though the older woman's was streaked with gray and she wasn't as tall as her robust daughter. "Sit right down—here, I'll take your hat," she said when I finally got back enough manners to remove it. "You sound like a Texas man to me. Kay tells me you've a plan to keep out the sheep."

"I don't know," I said, "if we can keep them out, but if we can talk your neighbors into going for this it just might make them easier to deal with."

"We'll hope so," she smiled. "Kay seems to set a lot of store by you. I understand you're acquainted with this man Rabas."

"Fact is, I've never actually laid eyes on the feller but I have had occasion to study his methods."

We spent the rest of the meal over small talk, most of it coming from the girl and her mother. As we were about to get up, Mrs. Wilbur asked, "Are you going to invite the Boxed O to this conference?"

"Hadn't figured to."

"Don't you think perhaps you should? Don't you think it might deter Mr. Rabas from—"

"The only thing," I said, "that will deter his kind is a gun in the gut and a plumb ready finger."

The girl pulled me away from her mother's shocked

face, grabbed up my hat and hustled me out before the old lady could collect scattered wits. On the porch she cried, "Did you have to say that?" Her eyes were near black with the outrage behind them. "Don't you care what folks think?"

"She asked me a question. I gave her the truth."

Kay said with pale cheeks, "Don't you want *any* friends?"

"What talent I have isn't geared in that direction. What I want's to get down to the business in hand. Sooner we know where we stand, the better I'll be able to deal with those sheep and the Injun gun slingers Rabas sends with them. If they latch onto your range, they'll take over your water. And without water, missy, your goose is cooked."

Outside the bunkhouse, which I could see across the yard, two of her hands held down a bench against the wall while the other pair squatted, rolling smokes, nearby. I didn't wait to follow her over but struck off forthwith.

Pulled up where I had all four of them in front of me, I said flat out, "My name's McGrath. I've hired on as range boss. I don't mind a bit of grousing but when I give an order I expect to be obeyed. Not tomorrow but straight off. If there's anyone here don't hold with that notion he better step up and draw his time right now."

They stared back at me in silence, nobody making any move to get up. They looked a pretty average lot, three of them younger than me and one older. Kay Wilbur stopped alongside of me while the quiet got quieter and I couldn't help wondering if the whole push would slope first time my back was turned.

"All right," I growled. "We've got a deal worked up that just might give this end of the cactus some hope of beating Rabas if he figures on pushing those sheep in again. Rocking Arrow will share this with any local outfit except Boxed O. Get the word passed around, all interested parties to be here tomorrow night. About nine o'clock, say."

As the men went off to mount up and get at it, Kay Wilbur, plainly not sold on this yet, said, "Fair is fair. On what kind of basis are we handing out shares?"

"On the number of cows in each of these brands. One share in Rocking Arrow to every twenty head."

"And what about their layouts—buildings and equipment, the horses packing their brands?"

"All thrown in along with the cattle." I could sense in her frown most of the objections I would hear. The rub in this she voiced straight off.

"Debarra—and Hardigan, too, I expect—isn't going to find that arrangement equitable. They've a lot more in buildings and overhead than the greasy sackers running thirty to forty cows in this Basin."

"Granted. On the other hand, though, there's a lot more of these two-bit outfits. The big thing you've got to look at is the territory covered—"

"And what about the plasters? More than half of those outfits are mortgaged to the hilt."

"No sweat there. Rocking Arrow, naturally, assumes their indebtedness."

"I think the bank may have something to say about—"

"The bank, as things stand, hasn't a Chinaman's chance of ever getting their money, and these spreads—as you've said your own self—are a drug on the market. They'll jump at the chance to get their hooks into the kind of an outfit we'll be putting together. Who's the bank's lawyer and where do I find him?"

"Barnabe Conrado. He's got an office in Sunflower." She considered me doubtfully, chewing her lip.

"There anything wrong with him?"

"No. It's just that . . . don't you think it might be better to get somebody who isn't so closely tied—"

"We haven't the time to shop around for a lawyer. What's good for us will be good for the bank. If we can pull this off, the bank will be paid. As it stands, right now they'll be lucky to get five cents on the dollar." I looked up at the sun. "I better get whacking. If I'm not back tonight, I'll see you tomorrow."

I was heading for the stable when she called after me. "What do you expect to be using for money?"

"We'll worry about that when the need catches up with us."

VIII

Because I had not been able to get all my chores tended as fast as I'd have liked, it was well after dark before I'd been able to shake off the dust of Sunflower and once again point my horse in the direction of Rocking Arrow.

I'd made no attempt to contact Shannon; there'd have been no point in it anyway. My role was plain. He wanted hell prized up and a chunk slipped under it.

I did get a look at that redheaded marshal. Twice he went by me without so much as the flick of an eyewinker. And he was again in plain sight when I came down the stairs from Conrado's office.

The bank's lawyer had been about as garrulous as the proverbial clam. He agreed to be present at the Rocking Arrow Invitational and allowed he'd be prepared to draw up any needed papers, promising to handle another chore for me.

But he could not be drawn as regards the feasibility of the merger I'd outlined. Though I got the impression he took a rather dim view of its prospects for success, so far anyway as blocking Rabas was concerned, I did by dint of considerable prodding get him to admit he foresaw no grounds for objections from the bank.

"Of course, this order you want me to telegraph on behalf of Rocking Arrow," he said in his mouth-puckered dry and fusty manner, "can have no financial connection with the bank. You understand that, don't you?"

"I certainly don't expect them to send good money after bad."

"Is the ranch going to open an account with the bank?"

"Guess you've played a few hands of poker," I told him, sourly regarding that half shut pair of eyes. "If we latch onto any spare change, we'll get in touch with them."

"You do that," he said. "And don't forget to keep in mind the indebtedness you incur by taking these fellows in must be held as a lien against Miss Wilbur's property."

"Against the property and chattels of the Rocking Arrow syndicate."

"That's right."

I didn't reckon his precious bank would allow us to forget. After quitting his office, I looked for a place to wet my whistle, figuring to give Major Shannon's pet marshal a chance to say whatever he aimed to. Recalling Frelton, the faro dealing barkeep, I hunted the street for the Buffalo Bull. Not finding that name on any of the signs, I turned into the hash house where Durphey had found me and settled for pie and java instead. But Durphey did not follow me in.

The clock on the wall said it was ten-fifteen. I debated getting a room for the night but, deciding against this, went back to the stable and bailed out my horse. He'd been watered and fed and while he'd likely been just as well pleased to catch a few winks, I guessed another trip under saddle wouldn't kill him. It wasn't that I was in any hurry to get back; I just couldn't see paying for the privilege of wasting a sleepless night on a skreaky bed in that stuffy hotel room.

I didn't push the pace none. I had a lot of notions I wanted to sort out and the sun had been up pretty near half an hour when I rode into the yard at Rocking Arrow and saw a man standing on the Wilbur house gallery.

It was a wide and bulky shadow he threw against the wall and I looked him over with the thoroughness of habit. He was big as I was, a little heavier maybe, with blue-black jowls on a face showing teeth in a thin and watchful smile.

I went on toward the day pen and was hoisting my rig to plop it on the top pole when this fellow sauntered up and stood with bold eyes rummaging my gear. I set the blanket over my saddle, hair side up to dry, slipped off the bridle and turned the gelding into the corral. "Something I can do for you?" I asked, looping the bridle over the horn.

He didn't speak straightaway, just kept looking me over. Kind of made me feel like a freak in a sideshow. Yet to be here that early taking his ease on the ranch house gallery gave him most of the earmarks of an overnight guest.

"So you're Pete McGrath," he said to me finally, "the bad man from Texas." And, when I didn't rise to that, "Aren't you bein' just a mite overconfident, throwing your weight around the way you been doin' with all of them badge toters scourin' the range?"

I didn't care for his patronizing scrutiny or the self-assurance he wore like a coat. By look and sound you'd have supposed this was *his* place. "If it bothers you," I said, "don't feel tied to my vicinity."

His big-nosed face tipped back in a laugh. "I guess you live up to your billing all right. I heard how you humbled Telesco."

It didn't sound like a compliment. I don't guess he meant it to. As I started to shove past he put out a hand. "Let me give you a little tip, McGrath. Don't sit so tall in the saddle. We've got along pretty well around here without your help."

I peered at him coldly. "You got something to say, get it off your chest."

His stare came back with a half humorous attention. He was obviously turning the remark over in his head, yet even now he appeared more amused than bothered.

This surprised me a little. It tightened the hold my feet had on the yard. "Man on the run," he threw at me lazily, "can't afford to stay very long in one place. You oughta think about that before you shove Kay's hopes up too high."

"You talk too much," I said to him softly, and saw those odd amber eyes of his quicken, but still he didn't altogether catch fire.

"You making a demonstration for—"

"When I demonstrate something, you'll get the message, believe me."

Laughing again, he turned on his heel and went sauntering carelessly back toward the house. I swore under my breath, remembering the stubbornness that lay along the forward throw of that jaw. Whoever he was, I would probably hear more of him. With that kind of talk it seemed pretty plain he did not have my best interest at heart. Which could complicate things if he decided to tip off the Texas authorities to my present whereabouts.

No two-bit greasy sacker with a handful of crossbred cattle tucked away someplace at the back of beyond was like to be throwing that sort of gab at any broke-out convict sent up for murder. He sure as hell was no Spaniard. So he had to be Hardigan, the man whose spread abutted the far side of Telesco.

Rather grimly, I wondered if they'd made a connection. My experience said it was not in the cards for a Rabas man to be in this Basin for the length of time Telesco had been holding the deed to Boxed O without putting in a few licks for his master. No one with sense to pound sand down a rat hole had to look at this big-nosed pelican twice to know he'd be stuffed to the gills with ambition.

I headed for the bunkhouse, figuring I'd better get some shut-eye. And knew before I pulled open the door things had come to a pretty slack pass in this outfit when a crew could be sleeping with the sun up this long. I jerked the first hand I come to plumb out of his bunk.

He hit the floor with a howl that shook the rest of them awake. "On your feet, all of you!" I said, holding hard to the heels of my temper. "If you got nothing to do I'll find something for you!" There were only three of them in this shack; two, looking sheepish, began to haul on their boots. "Where's that other bird?"

The man on the floor got up, rubbing a shoulder. He appeared some put out but buttoned his lip after a scowl at my face. One of the others, peering round with surprise, said, "Rittenhouse?" and shrugged. "Guess he ain't back yet."

It was the oldest hand that was missing.

The third puncher, getting into his vest, offered: "Old Ritt's the one went to Squaw Butte after Debarra—had a couple of others to ask on the way."

I looked them over. "How come coosie didn't rouse you for grubpile?"

Man in the vest said, "Rittenhouse is cook. He had a pretty dry ride. Might of stopped off in town." The other pair swapped glances.

"That his regular habit?"

When no one else spoke, the one I'd roughed up,

with my eyes hard upon him, growled, "He does like a nip or two now an' again."

I wheeled for the door. "Find yourselves something to do. Something useful," I said, and struck out for the corrals.

I got the rope off my saddle and hauled out a big grulla, a mouse-colored gelding that stacked up to have a lot of miles he'd been hoarding. I threw my gear on and got into the saddle. Kay Wilbur came out of the house waving as I turned into the yard. "Are you headed for town?"

"I been thinking some about it."

"Do you mind picking up a few items at the store?"

"What sort of items and how do I pay for them?"

Ignoring my clipped tone she handed up a list. "Just put them on my bill," she said, "and while you're there, get yourself a new hat. No cow boss I ever knew would be caught dead in that thing you're wearing."

She said it cold sober with no hint of a grin.

It put a face in my head and I looked steamily past her the length of the gallery but Hardigan—if he had put her up to this—was cannily keeping himself out of sight. I said to her, "Yes, ma'am," and rode from the yard with one more reason why no one with the brains God give to a gopher would ever be fool enough to work for a woman.

IX

The morning turned out to be a real sizzler with the sun beating down from almost straight overhead when the Rocking Arrow grulla fetched me into the top o Bad News' single street. The ride had not greatly im proved my outlook nor much tempered the opinion had formed of Lee Hardigan.

Going over my impressions as the miles unreeled, it had seemed rather likely the fellow showed more than a passing interest in the affairs of the spread I was presumably working for.

Was Hardigan courting Kay Wilbur? I recollected the flush she had flown at his mention and wryly wondered if it was her or her ranch that had first place in his parade of attentions. Either way he'd be a nuisance, and doubly so if she imagined herself to be in love with the fellow.

I suppose he had a certain animal magnetism. The bold sure way of taking things for granted plus that sleepy-lidded stare might well appeal to the romantic streak in women, especially a girl like Kay, tucked away on a ranch at the back of beyond with few normal contacts and no father to look after her.

I didn't see how jealousy could have any part in what I felt about him. He had nothing I coveted and, certainly, nobody wearing Pete McGrath's boots had any business getting steamed up over some hank of hair. I had long since put such weaknesses away from me.

The curvaceous Kay had nothing to do with this.

It had to go back to those cat-colored stares, to some half caught glimpse of corrosion deep smoldering behind those twisted grins he poker-faced paraded after the manner of a bull killer flapping his cape to hide away things he didn't want examined. The marks of a man too given to short measure.

I piled off my horse in front of the store, slapped the reins over the pole and, ducking under it, went up the steps to push inside and lay Kay's list on the counter. "I'll be after this stuff in about half an hour."

"Just a minute there, mister. This here for Rocking Arrow?"

I reckoned he must have seen my set-to with Telesco;

there was no other way he could have placed me so surely unless he had read the brand on my horse. "What about it?"

"Afraid it'll have to be cash on the barrelhead."

"I understood we had an account at this store."

Behind his counter the aproned man said with nervous defiance, "I've got to live, too. It'll be cash or no groceries."

"You want to bite on that?" I growled, placing on the scarred wood a gold double eagle.

He looked like I'd tossed a live rattler between us. "Be damn sure it's ready when I'm ready for it."

Back on the street, I looked for the deadfall I had seen here before. Its batwings weren't thirty feet from my horse; now I saw something I hadn't noticed in the dark. A long while ago some itinerant painter had daubed its name in foot high letters clean across the front. Badly flaked and faded, they still spelled out the words BUFFALO BULL.

It rang in my head some kind of a bell but we all make mistakes of one kind or another. Too riled to heed its tinkle of warning, I crossed the road and stepped half blind into a quality of quiet no man hears but once without forever remembering.

To my sun-filled eyes, it was like a veil had been hung between where I'd stopped and that smoke darkened bar. I could vaguely make out what looked like four shapes, a pair of them just this side of the mahogany, the two others stiffened above kicked-back chairs at a table that showed the top half of another sprawled limply across it.

"*You won't be so goddam lucky this time!*" cried a hate ragged voice.

It had to be him. No one but a tinhorn fool would waste his chance in footless gab—even with a gun laid on me. I whipped around, twisting, and drove two shots straight into the flare of that smoke wreathed pistol, and saw his mouth stretch wide in a yell that went unheard in the jar and jump of those hammering explosions.

The gun fell out of his flopped-open fist and he looked all jaw and goggling eyes as the hinges of his knees let go and spilled him onto the sawdust strewn floor.

In the wavering light of the coal-oil lamps no one else in that dive moved so much as a finger till Frelton's woman drew a shuddery breath and, crossing herself, said: "He sure as hell asked for it!"

I looked at the shape sprawled across the table and saw it was Rittenhouse, stoned to the gills. The burly pair by the chairs were not riding men: they didn't have the legs or the clothes of cowhands—lumberjacks probably. They stood watching me, ugly, not two breaths removed from taking this up where Frelton had dropped it. Only the gun in my fist held them quiet.

When the girl started forward, the nearest one said, "Keep out of this, Angie."

I twisted my lip at them. "They're not passing out harps where Frelton went, boys, but there's plenty of room if you want to find out."

"If you've come for that slob, you won't never make it."

"I'll make it," I said. "Bring his horse around, Angie."

I could feel her eyes. Then her heels went tap-tapping toward the bar's end, forty feet from the swing doors that gave on the street.

The nearest lumberjack grinned. They weren't either of them armed, but they knew well as I did I would have my work cut out getting Rittenhouse over my shoulder and keeping them covered all the while I was doing it. It simply wasn't in the cards.

"All right, you two. Pick him up," I said.

Neither one of them budged. They were betting I wouldn't cut them down in cold blood. Or maybe they were stalling till reinforcements could get here. I could cripple them of course, but there'd been more racket already than I'd have chosen.

They were both grinning now.

It was beginning to look like a Mexican standoff when Angie said from behind the bar: "Unless you're fixing to ignore this Greener, you two varmints better do as invited." There was a metallic double click as she cocked both hammers. "Real pronto."

Those boys were tough but you could see them blanch. Only a plumb idiot would think to cross a nervous female with a sawed-off in her hands.

They got Rittenhouse out of his chair, got the wobbly legs straightened under him and steered him toward the batwings. They were meek right now as just dropped lambs but how they would feel when those doors shut behind us, cutting off Angie's view and the threat of that Greener, took a lot of getting used to. But Frelton's woman was way ahead of me.

She was already out from behind the bar, keeping pace with them, step for step, and went through the batwings right on their heels.

"You're doing just fine, boys. I'd hate to see you fall down now," she said as, gun lifted, I pushed through behind them. "That bright bay is his. Tie him into the saddle."

Which was when I remembered the stuff I was supposed to pick up at the store. If I didn't pack it out to the ranch with me now, those folks I'd invited to set in on this powwow might feel hospitality was in short supply. But if I left these bruisers to go over there now almost anything could happen.

Yet I had to go over there to get my horse.

I said to Frelton's woman: "Don't suppose you've seen Telesco around, have you?"

Something passed through the turn of her eyes like doubt, then her face ironed out to reply coolly thoughtful, "He took off in a hurry right after this slumbum mentioned that meeting you been asking folks to."

X

While I stood digesting this, the burly timberman working with Rittenhouse—who wasn't armed, either—got him roped over the saddle like a sack of grain. He'd have a sore gut tomorrow I thought, and wondered why I was bothering with him when what I had really ridden in to prevent was that bit of information he had already leaked.

What I ought to do was go after Telesco, but before I could make up my mind Angie said, "If it's work you're hunting—"

"I've got a job now."

She said with a skeptical lift of her brows, "I'm talking about work you'd get paid cash money for. Frelton had a half interest in this place. Now he's gone, it comes to me." She let me think about that. "Why tie yourself up to an outfit that's going to be out of business by this time next month?"

The real answer to that sat in a second floor office like a spider back in Sunflower. I wasn't about to tell her. Nor get into any longwinded gab swap. "I don't like working for a woman," I said gruffly.

"You're working for one now. What's that uppity Wilbur got you couldn't get from me?—plus real, hard spendable coin of the realm." She swiveled her eyes in a reproving look at the lumberjack pair standing by the cribbed pole. "Don't let idle hands steer you into mischief, boys. If this thing goes off they'll be picking up pieces of you all the way to Dover."

She grinned at their scowls, swung her glance back to me. "Two hundred a month I'll pay you, McGrath, and who could say fairer than that? Are you on?"

A woman scorned was a damn poor risk with her lily white hands wrapped around that Greener. "Who's your partner?" I said, fishing round for something that might bulwark my turndown.

"Why do you reckon I'd give such a bundle if it wasn't for needing to make sure he stays honest? I like the cut of your jib, McGrath. You've already handled him once with real style."

Of course, I thought. *Telesco*. It had to be.

She was watching me, trying to catch at the notions wheeling through my head, trying to gauge my reaction from inscrutable cheeks. Past her shoulder I saw the man who'd tied Rittenhouse step toward the tail of the unconscious cook's horse. It was no time to gamble. I said: "One more move and you can reach for a halo."

Angie's head whipped around. I wrenched the shotgun away from her, jumping back to forestall any retaliatory tantrum she might launch to regain it.

I took her measure right then when she dropped the sweet from her voice to swear like a Mexican bootshine boy. She had the kind of a tongue would take off flesh clean down to the bone, but I managed to keep one eye on my business. I told the woodsy pair by the pole to strike out. "So long, boys," I said. "Straight off down the road and if you value your health keep right on hiking."

They knew which side of the bread got the butter. Neither one of them stopped for a second invitation.

"Much obliged for your help," I said in Angie's direction and, picking up the bay's reins, struck off across the road to pick up my own. "I'll leave your hardware at the store," I told her over my shoulder, and saw the storekeeper goggling from the edge of his stoop.

He backed off, ducked inside and came out with a tow sack gripped in his fist as I was drawing the loads from her broke-open Greener.

"You catch on fast," I told him, putting the gun down and taking the sack to tie it back of the saddle. "Give my regards to all inquiring friends."

It was mid-afternoon when I got back to the ranch. Hardigan's horse was in one of the corrals but no one came out when I pulled up by the bunkhouse, untied the limp cook, eased him off the saddle and shouldered him in. Having no idea which of these was his bunk, I dumped him into the first one I came to. I freed the sackful of groceries, took both animals for a snort at the trough then hauled them over to a stand by the day pen while I got the gear off them. I stood a moment watching them roll, then put up the bars, went back for the tow sack and wrestled it across to plop it down by the door on the gallery planking.

"Is that you?" Kay asked, coming to stare through the screen.

I said, blowing my cheeks out, "What's left of me, I guess," and saw the odd look she gave me.

"You didn't have any trouble, did you?"

"I didn't lose any hide. You've run out of credit at the store, though," I told her. "Hereafter it's got to be cash—I paid for this stuff. Eat hearty."

I didn't wait for whatever might have been in her mind. I steered my spurs across the yard and went into the fumes and drunken snores of the bunkhouse, where the day's trapped heat was like the breath from a furnace. Too beat to think about the needs of my belly, I hauled off my boots, got my shoulders out of the sweat-damp shirt and spread myself out on the one stripped bunk.

It was racket made by the returning crew that fetched me back to the land of the quick. Knuckling sleep stuck eyes, I pushed myself up and sat there a spell trying to pull myself together. First thing I thought about like usual was Gold Spur Charlie and the bastardly way I'd been cheated of revenge. Somebody poked his head in the door, took just enough time for a good second look and backed out in a hurry.

I suppose I looked like the wrath of God.

Stamping into my boots I got up and looked out. It was dusk outside and there were lights in the house. A couple strange nags stood on dropped reins before the gallery and a black horse stood between the shafts of a buggy somewhat nearer to the door. The rig, I reckoned, probably belonged to the bank's Sunflower lawyer, Conrado. Who the saddlers belonged to was anybody's guess.

I can't remember why but I dug out the note I'd got about Charlie, took it over to a window for another scowling look. Nothing had been added. It still said the same but I saw something now I hadn't realized before. My informant hadn't bothered to sign his name.

It set me thinking. I don't know why this should have bothered me. The writer could have had any number of reasons for not wanting to be identified. Yet that lack of a signature stuck in my craw, opening up as it did the whole can of worms. How had this fellow known I was interested in Charlie? And how had he known where to send his damned note?

That lack of a name made the whole deal suspect.

I found myself sweating as my thoughts leaped around like a boxful of crickets. That goddam message could be a hoax! If Charlie'd known I'd broke prison he would probably have guessed I'd be after him—he had to figure I would, no matter how Injun clever he had covered his tracks. A guilty conscience had made cowards out of tougher hands than Charlie.

The son of a bitch could have sent that note himself!

Approaching steps slanched my glance toward the door. The bulk of a shape pretty near blocked out what was left of the light. "You in there, McGrath?"

Hardigan's voice.

Remembering him without pleasure, I growled.

He said with a hint of a grin in his tone, "Boss wants you over to the house. On the double."

"You been put on the payroll?"

Hardigan laughed. "Way *I* heard, this outfit can't even pay for its groceries."

"You got the longest ears of any wolf I know."

"I been round this country a fortnight or two—"

"You could be around permanent you keep on like you're going."

"That any way for a hired hand to yap at the feller that's about to be his boss' chief partner?"

Behind the aggrieved tone of voice he'd adopted there was still that thin edge of saturnine amusement. I said, "You sound pretty happy for a gent getting ready to stake out an interest in a leaky ship."

"Leaks can be plugged. I figure Rocking Arrow can rock along quite a spell," he tossed back smugly, "Once we get rid of the excess ballast."

I stared, darkly thinking. "You got something up your sleeve I haven't looked at yet?"

"You'll be hearing about it before the night's out." He swung away from the door.

Before he had gone three steps I flung after him, "Some kinds of ballast can give a gent a rupture if he ain't braced proper when he bends to lift."

Hardigan's laugh floated back through the dark. "You better look at your hole card."

XI

I caught up my hat with a headful of questions and was bound for the door when the feel of my face put a match in my hand. I found what I sought against the far wall, a cracked and fly-speckled piece of mirror held with bracket screws above a small ledge. I peered at my mug with even less regard than I could generally afford.

Somebody's straight-edge lay folded on the shelf and, snuffing the flame, I picked this up. I was moving toward the corrals when a jumble of gab coming out of the cookshack drew me over to the lamplit windows. The hands were all in there stuffing their faces. They glanced up at my entrance but none of them spoke.

I got me a plate and helped myself from the stove, caring very little if they liked me or not. I sat down at the empty head of the table, hearing the wind fall away, bothered even less that my presence could so effectively dry up their talking talents. One by one they got through and departed, dropping their tools in the wreck pan en route. I was used to my company, these saddle pounders weren't.

When a man steps beyond what his peers regard as normal, one can hardly expect to be comfortable around him. Whatever these boys had been told about me, they were bound to have heard some hopped-up version of my run-in with Telesco. That in itself would have set me apart.

But a man who has killed undergoes inescapably certain changes which—while perhaps not apparent— are frequently reflected in his traffic with others. He's been hardened or toughened and this kind of thing is felt. There is no middle ground. Either you're drawn to such a person or you tend to avoid him.

I could live with it. I hadn't come to make friends. I was here to sow discord, my mission diversion. The major wasn't interested in means, only the product. And about this time I found myself wondering if maybe this wasn't also Hardigan's intention. If it was, I thought dryly, we could be in for a rather lively session here tonight.

Someway, though, the man didn't strike me as the kind to be interested in doing things for others. Any chestnuts he might engage to retrieve would be strictly for Hardigan's own account. He might be teamed up with others but whatever he did would be done for himself.

Something else that kept scratching me was by what means he had managed to hitch my name to the proper background. Any close-mouthed stranger with the earmarks of travel, drifting into a cow country this time of year, could be suspected by some folks of being on the dodge. But this wasn't an assumption on Hardigan's part. He had straight off labeled me "the bad man from Texas." How had he pinned me down so quick?

And he'd been equally blunt in his roughshod suggestion Kay could get along nicely without my help. He would know by now I'd no intention of letting mere words drive me off, so what was he figuring to do about me? Tip off the authorities? Turn me in for the bounty Texans had put up?

He wouldn't do it for the money but I reckoned he wasn't above taking it.

Getting up from the table, I rummaged around till I found the bucket of "soft" soap coosie used in the wreck pan. It was yellow and thick—like lard to the touch, and strong enough to take the hide off a town dude. I scooped up a gob and with the razor in my pocket struck out for the corrals.

I had in mind a bath and shave but passed up the day pen, closest to the house, in favor of the privacy of one not made so public by light from the lamps.

On the rim of the trough I scraped the soap from my hand, pulled off my boots, unbuckled the shellbelt and got out of my clothes. The water in these tanks was spring-fed and cold. Displacing quite a splash of it, I got in, scooted down, drawing my knees up till nothing but their knobs and my hatted head was above the surface. I must have lay there soaking the best part of ten minutes.

I was like that, luxuriating, when a sound of approaching steps dragged my head around. Belatedly remembering I was wanted at the house, I was scrabbling around to get hold of my pistol in case this was Hardigan tracking me down when Kay's voice called, "Are you out there, McGrath?"

Well, Jesus Christ!

There I was, bare ass naked, and her by the sound not ten steps away! No frog ever got under water half as fast—nor came out any quicker or with half as much noise as me . . . plumb forgetting to shut my damn trap.

I must have lowered that trough by nigh onto two gallon, and—coughing, spluttering, trying to get it out of me, at least enough to have a little room left for air—that was where she found me, doubled over, gasping like a half drowned rat.

I don't know how much she could see in that dark but the next thing I recall being sure enough aware of she'd come right up and was pounding my back like hell wouldn't have it.

No "September Morn" could have been anything like as put out and ringy as Pete McGrath time I finally got rid of her. Dealing with a crisis without any clothes on—and a female crisis at that, is pretty near enough to drive a man to drink. Time she left, I was overdue and ready to hit anything that got in my way.

Time I was dressed and crossing the yard it must have been within spitting distance of the hour I had set for those invited to be on hand. There were more horses now racked in front of the gallery. I cut over to the bunkhouse where Rittenhouse's snores told me how much good I was like to get out of him. I stood there a moment, swapping stares with the others.

Singling out the skinniest kid, I told him to arm himself with a rifle and be prepared to stand off invaders. Bidding the other pair follow, I struck out for the house.

I could feel their unspoken questions and appreciate the nag of curiosity these boys were wrestling with but judged they would a lot better stay on their toes if left to simmer along with the rest. However, I said as we approached the gallery, "Take a squint at these broncs and let me know who's not here."

All were present who'd been asked but three of the two-bit outfits.

When we got inside, I took a quick look around. Eight men—not counting Hardigan—were crowded into the Rocking Arrow parlor, six of them gents I had never seen before. The two exceptions were Conrado, the lawyer, and a little wart of a jasper in run-over heels that, the last time I'd noticed, had been bossing a livery on the San Saba outskirts. Gurley his name was.

I didn't think it likely, despite the phlegmatic look he sloshed past me, a man his age would forget the caught gun who'd rubbed out the town banker.

Kay Wilbur, getting up from where she'd been sitting alongside her mother, said, "This is Pete McGrath, the

Rocking Arrow foreman. You've been asked here to listen to a proposition he's come up with which he thinks may keep a lot of you afloat and—"

"I'll take it from there," I growled, cutting in, and set my back hard against the door. "You boys all run cows in this Basin. Most of you, as things stand right now, will be wiped out if Rabas and his sheep come in here again. I happen to know this is what they intend; they'll not only come but are figuring to stay."

I let them jaw a while on that, paying no attention to the questions being shot my way. When some of the wind had abated a little, I said, like Moses handing down the ten tablets: "You tried last year to handle these people on a community basis . . . which has never worked anyplace. Sometimes with sheep a deadline's the answer but this feller Rabas is a new breed to most. He comes prepared. He's big enough to laugh at you. Big enough to bury Wilbur and go right on laughing to the next batch of cow nurses that fondly imagine he's got to find some way around them.

"When are you knotheads going to wake up? When he has to go round a thing, Rabas don't come within gunshot of it."

Giving this notion time to percolate, I got out the makings and rolled up a quirly. Putting fire to it, I let narrowed eyes play over their faces, noting particularly Hardigan's smugness and the poker-cheeked look of San Saba's ex-liveryman.

"Which brings us," I said, "to why you been asked here. This spread's still in business. We're going to keep it that way, thanks to the wells Wilbur dug through these hills. We're considering right now the possibilities of a syndicate. Increasing its size may not keep out Rabas, but it will force him to scrap any plans he's firmed up. It will make us a lot harder nut to crack. And you can all get under Rocking Arrow's umbrella, get a piece of this partnership—a stake in the outfit—by dropping your holdings into the pot."

XII

There could hardly have been any greater commotion had I been Chicken Little with her outrageous notion that the skies were about to fall. All over the room men were jumping up, shouting, trying to drown out their neighbors, each vociferously expounding his own views, nobody taking any time out to listen till the bank's Sunflower mouthpiece, Barnabe Conrado, in all his Victorian elegance, looked at me and threw up his hands with an eloquence that would have done justice even to a Disraeli.

I pounded the wall with the butt of my six-shooter. When I got enough attention to make talking profitable, I said into the racket, "You don't have all night to make up your minds."

Hardigan, no doubt thinking this would settle it, wanted to know in his hog-calling manner on what basis partnerships would be taken.

"On the basis of cows," I said through the rumble. "For every ten cows, their owner gets one share of Rocking Arrow stock."

A calculating quiet spread through the room across which the portly moustachioed Mex asked, "Por favor. Por these we geef up all we 'ave? Our ranch? Brand? Our cabalos? Beside *vacas?*"

"That's right. Mr. Conrado here will draw up the papers."

"Not mine, he won't!" someone angrily shouted, and the hubbub broke out again, refreshed by indignation.

Then Gurley said, when he could make himself heard: "What about that money we owe at the bank?"

"The Rocking Arrow syndicate assumes your obligations."

"That's good enough for me," said Gurley, and three-four other two-bit owners glumly nodded.

"And the mortgage-free spreads have to take the same deal?"

That was Hardigan, brows up, putting in his oar. "There don't none of you *have* to do anything," I said. "If you want to stay out of this combine, more power to you—though where it will come from *I* don't know."

"You don't know that joining will keep Rabas out, either," Hardigan growled. "You don't even *know* he'll come anywhere near here!"

I said, without beating around any bushes, "I'd give something to know whose side you're on."

"I'm not backing any sheep, you can be sure of that." His beefy cheeks took on color. When he realized others were staring at him, too, he pushed a laugh across his teeth. "I didn't suppose my politics were open to question." With his pale eyes swiveling, he declared with some vigor: "I stand where I've always stood, squarely with the majority."

This didn't, to me, appear to say very much. He had a flair for talking all around a thing without ever touching the meat of a subject.

"Then why," I asked, "are you bucking this deal?"

"I don't know that I am. I like to know where I stand is all. First thing we ought to be told, seems to me, is how much say the new partners will have."

"Each partner will have one vote for each share."

Hardigan looked down his nose. "Won't that put all decisions between Miss Wilbur and Carlos Debarra? All the small-spread owners voting as a block couldn't begin to offset any policy—"

"As a man who believes in majority rule, don't you feel the people with the most to lose ought to have the most say?"

That caught him neatly between wind and water. While he was trying to scrape a way around that, I said to the rest of them, "Any of you gents that want in on this can line up over there by Mr. Conrado, who will put down your names, look into your titles and—as soon as we've gotten some kind of a count—give you whatever shares you've got coming."

Before anyone could more than get started, one of the two-bitters wanted to know who would be doing all the work for this oufit.

"We'll all be working, everyone of us," I said. "Hired hands, partners, the whole push will work, some in one capacity, some in another—there'll be no idle hands, you can bank on that."

Hardigan swung round and headed for the lawyer—Gurley and several of the others trailing after him. I thought to have glimpsed as he turned away some hint or return of that sly gloating smugness which had seemed so markedly prevalent earlier.

There was just about time to take a hard look when over his shoulder like pearls before pigs he chucked the pronouncement he'd been hugging all evening. "May show you where I stand in this business to learn Miss Wilbur and myself very shortly are figuring to be sharing what is known as double harness."

In the thunderstruck exchange of whipped-about glances, Debarra—first to break out of that galvanized hush—demanded with some asperity to be told if this signified an intention to marry.

"You couldn't be righter," Hardigan told him, while Kay, prettily flushing, shyly nodded her head.

Debarra, plainly affronted, said moving doorward

with darkening cheeks, "You can do this without my cows and my horses. Don't count on me to have any part in it."

"Just a minute," I said, still blocking the door. Understanding very well what had got in his craw, I said for the record, "Exactly what do you object to?"

"I'm tired of being victimized by gringo tricks!"

"Tricks?" I said. "You call marriage a trick?"

He waved this away with the flat of a hand. "Words!" he spat with a palpable contempt. "I am not a fool to be so easily deceived! On the day Miss Wilbur becomes Mrs. Hardigan, no one else in this syndicate will have any say at all! Have the kindness, señor, to step away from the door."

More than half those riled faces had whipped around to peer at Hardigan. "If that's what's in his mind," I said, "he'll have to shorten his rope a bit. This pool's my notion. Until this business of Rabas is settled, as syndicate ramrod I'll call the tune."

There was an obvious answer to that and it was equally obvious from Hardigan's silence he knew what it was but could not use it without tipping his hand. To say flat out that I was replaceable would be to confirm all Debarra's suspicions and kill the last hope of support from the rest of them.

But Debarra was under no such restraint. He said with curled lip: "When he picks up the Wilbur shares by this marriage, the first thing he'll do will be to get rid of you!"

The ex-liveryman, Gurley, spoke out to say dryly, "Maybe. I'll string my bets with McGrath any day."

Another wheeling of stares held the small owners rooted while the quiet spread in ripples to every corner of the room. I didn't want this testimonial, too gripped by what might be easily involved if it came out in this bickering how the boss he supported was a man-killing fugitive. Hardigan could use that any time he'd a mind to. No one had to tell Hardigan. He already knew.

But I didn't think he'd told Kay yet. I wondered why he hadn't. He didn't look the kind that would pull any punches.

He went on toward Conrado, followed by Gurley with three nervous others moving drag-footed after him —prodded more by the weight of unpayable debts than any real conviction.

One of those who had not joined this procession wanted to know how I figured to keep Rabas out of an open range country. "By your own tell," he growled, "them rifle packin' Injuns'll run over any deadline set up."

"They're sure not the kind to try playing games with."

"How you goin' to keep 'em outa here then?"

I said, watching Hardigan's shoulders, "Hardest thing I know to keep is a secret shared. Guess you'll just have to take it on faith."

At least this whippoorwill was forthright enough. Straight from the shoulder he told all hands, "I'm not buyin' no damn pig in a poke!" and aimed for the door.

I got out of his way. Better to lose two or three I thought, than spread my cards where Hardigan could use my own scheme to unload me. He was probably saving me up for some badge toter.

Holding this back ought to anyways buy me a little more time. Unless he had already sold out to Rabas. Which I was less ready to believe now that he'd announced the inside track he'd got onto with Kay. With an edge like that, he should be more anxious than anyone else to keep Rocking Arrow away from those sheep.

As the squatter reached to pull open the door, the girl herself took chips in this deal. "I think," she said to him, "you're making a mistake. It stands to reason anyone not included will be a lot more vulnerable. By your-self you'll not have any chance at all, Giles."

"We'll see," the man growled, and slammed the door back of him.

XIII

"He'll head straight for Boxed O!" cried Hardigan, glaring.

"So what if he does? What can he tell that won't be all over by this time tomorrow?" I looked at Debarra. "You pulling out, too?"

The Mexican surprised me by shaking his head.

"How come?"

Debarra shrugged. "I can see now the wisdom in what you told Giles. Besides," he admitted with a twisted smile, "I could not hold back the sheep by myself."

Evidently his words convinced whichever owners had been still undecided. No one else left and I found my-self with considerable more room than I had honestly expected.

Recalling the boundaries I'd been shown on Kay's map, I thought—if Conrado had done what he'd agreed to—we had an even chance of keeping Rabas from be-coming the cat's-paw of those who saw ruin in Roose-velt's backing of the National Forests bill.

The sheep king, from what I had gathered, was a sight too canny to put his living and whole reputation on the line in a contest whose outcome could be made to seem dubious. His formidable shadow had come from a succession of frightening victories wrought from at first overconfident and then half demoralized bun-glers who had never really bothered to learn much about him.

My own sketchy strategy—taking these factors into account—was based on the flagged stick belief that a bluff built strong enough might solve our problem short of embracing any actual showdown, that the man would sooner go round than risk everything he'd achieved in a fight too unlikely to be resolved in his favor. He had more guts than you could hang on a fencepost but he wasn't a fool. I didn't think he would willingly unleash a holocaust he might not be able to get himself out of.

The combine, of course, would put a deal of pressure on him—this could be their last chance to open up more of the range closed to sheep but it didn't have to be *this* range. I figured Mr. Rabas to be smart enough to know this.

After the meeting broke up and Kay's new partners had quit the yard, I left her and Hardigan to walk Conrado out to his buggy. "Think you can hold them in line?" he asked skeptically. "You can't treat Debarra or that bullheaded Irishman with the bunched-up fist you'd use on the rest of them."

"I'm not worried about Debarra—"

"You should be. He's notional. He's a proud man, McGrath, who's had his pride too often stepped on to trust any Anglo out of his sight. If he pulls out—"

"Those agreements you had the bunch of them sign were supposed to be binding—'foolproof' you said. If you've left any loopholes—"

"They'll hold up in court. They're all hog-tied to this syndicate and, by the same token, they've all got a piece of it. You've got their livestock and whatever land they hold by tradition and usage, including water rights and patented acres. But there's no legal way you can prevent them from selling or even giving away their interest in this spread to somebody else. And that includes sheepmen."

He tapped my chest with a rigid finger. "If Debarra

—at the northeast edge of Rocking Arrow's new boundary—becomes for any reason disenchanted with you
or this fix you have put him in, you'll never hold him.
If he sells out to Rabas it will open a wedge—"

"I can take care of that."

"The bank will expect you to," the lawyer said dryly. "But the same thing applies even more aptly to
Hardigan. I know you don't think this likely, but ex-
pediency can make some very strange bedfellows. If
they bury their differences and *both* sell out, you'd
be left high and dry in the untenable position of having
sheep on both sides of you."

"Hardigan's too ambitious ever to swap a witch for
the devil. If I've got him pegged right, he's had this
place in his eye a heap too long to cut his string now,
after talking Kay into the prospect of marriage. He
may try other stunts but he won't sell out. The man's
too ambitious to cut his own throat."

Leaning toward me, Conrado lowered his voice con-
fidentially. "Without he's got more scruples than his
old man had, that girl will be in for a bad time with
him." With a grimace and another quick look about,
he said with his breath hot against my ear, "Did you
know Hardigan Senior was hanged for a horse thief?"

This Sunflower mouthpiece with his clothes and
garrulity could have stepped straight out of some old-
timey tintype. Baggy broadcloth trousers made by a
tailor that didn't quite meet the tops of high-buttoned
shoes no self-respecting cow nurse would have been
found dead in. Frilled lawn for a shirt. Lavender silk
for a cravat at his throat with his shoulders wedged into a clawhammer coat of the soot-colored kind most
favored by undertakers. Add to that a top hat like in
the pictures of Lincoln. Edge the cheeks with ginger
burnsides, put into the neck of Ichabod Crane an Adam's
apple that bobbed up and down like a gopher ducking

in and out of its hole, slap on the frayed blur of a frothy moustache and you'd have some notion of what I was looking at.

I said, "I guess we all have things to live down."

"Well, don't say you weren't warned. I've seen the way he looks at you. Don't ever wind up with your back to that feller."

He got into his buggy and drove away.

Food for thought's what they call it.

I didn't need him to underline for me the precariousness of what I hoped to do here. Nor did I need anyone to point out I hadn't been sent here to stave off trouble. It was beginning to look like I could have my hands full. If I failed to produce the full scale diversion that hardcased major had specifically ordered, I'd probably have him on my shirttail, too. Either way, it appeared highly probable my days as boss of this outfit were numbered.

Avoiding the parlor and the engaged couple's privacy, I went down the long hall, shouldered my warsack and was about to remove myself to the bunkhouse when the hand I had posted stepped out of the shadows, still lugging his rifle.

"You want I should stick here till Hardigan leaves?"

I'd plumb forgot about him and wondered how much he'd caught of my gab. Not that it made any great amount of difference. There was nothing I'd said in that talk with the lawyer that couldn't bear repeating. Anyone with half an eye could tell I wasn't overly high among Hardigan's choices for boss of this spread.

I shook my head. "You might's well get some sleep. That sport will probably stay on half the night."

"You want I should tell Joe to pound his ear, too?"

"I'll tell him," I said, and found him, rifle across knees, hunched on the top pole of one of the corrals.

"Ain't you afraid of a crick in the neck sleeping that way?" I asked. He come to with such a jerk he pretty near toppled himself off his perch. "You'll not fool owls or chickens no matter how long you roost there. Tomorrow's another day. Go on to bed. And be damn sure you roust out that cook before sunup."

I tossed down my sack and put my back to a gatepost.

A good time, I thought, to sort out a few facts from the treadmill of notions wheeling round through my head.

XIV

You might think I would be a heap more concerned, playing fast and loose with adamant orders hung round my neck by a government agent so closely placed to the indefatigable Teddy. I was edgy enough about this in all conscience.

The ubiquitous major was no guy to kick out a boot and yell boo at. But, despite his rep as a retriever of chestnuts—or maybe because of it—he'd picked up some bad habits and the newest was thinking he could bamboozle *me*.

I expect I was just being mule-headed stupid to be flying in the face of Providence that way, with the penalty paraded like a flung-down gauntlet in Shannon's growled threat to send me back to the rockpile. Way it looked to me, then, I was going to wind up there whether or not, unless some bullet settled my hash first. I didn't think Lee Hardigan would let much grass get to growing under him without taking steps to stop my clock.

It was mostly, I guess, in a spirit of dog-in-the-manger defiance that I had made up my mind to help this misfit bunch of ragtag ranchers—or maybe just the chance to get back at the sheep crowd who'd spawned with their own brand of arrogance such a mean-minded bastard as Gold Spur Charlie. I still couldn't think of that son of a bitch without all the bile piling up in my throat.

Not even to myself was I about to admit redheaded Kay Wilbur could have anything to do with it.

So now, with breakfast out of the way and the sun not yet clearing the tops of the Mazatzals, I was on my way with the half-asleep Joe to have a look at the lay-out Rabas had bought for the gunhand who went by the name of Telesco.

I was under no illusions at all about him. Despite any notions implied by our encounter in front of the Bad News store that day I had made Kay's acquaintance, it stood to reason this jasper was pretty strong medicine or Rabas wouldn't of had him around in the first place.

Joe, as our course straightened out toward Boxed O, began to show signs of an increasing uneasiness. He wasn't giving much attention to the steers and cows we passed and as we neared the north edge of Rocking Arrow's claimed range this jumpiness got the best of him. "You ain't figgerin', are you, to brace that cold-jawed Telesco again?"

"It kind of ran through my head."

"Then you better hev it looked at!" he declaimed, giving me the tone of voice generally reserved to fools and foreigners. "Ain't you been told what happened to High Henry, not half a mile from where we're settin' right now? That bunch ain't got a mite of friendliness in 'em!"

I grinned at the goggling look of his eyes. "When they told me you were staying on without pay I says,

'There's a man got guts enough to slap a full-growed bull in the face.'"

"Yeah," he said in a grudging fashion, "but that Telesco jigger ain't no damn bull."

"He looks just as two-legged human as any other knucklehead that would spend all his time with a bunch of blatting woolies. Wouldn't it pleasure you to get in a few licks for old Henry?"

"Well, but—"

"I been called a lot of things here and there but nobody's ever proved I was careless." I told him about the cow pool we'd started, the expansion of range this would bring Rocking Arrow. "We've got to know more about this Boxed O—how many hands they can put in the saddle—stuff like that. It was Rabas, not him, put the dough in that spread."

He peered toward the hills and the troughs that wound back to those out-of-sight buildings. "I wouldn't," he said, "want to git in your way."

"Don't you mind about that. You've got a reason for being here."

"I hev?" Astonishment didn't take the scowl off his face. "How'd you dig that up?"

"Simple arithmetic. When those fellers signed up to take shares in this outfit," I said, putting my horse into motion again, "the crew—by the terms laid down for this deal—grew like them beans Jack's ma threw out the window."

Took him a while but he worked his way through it. Said, eyes rounding: "We're a *big* outfit now?"

"Any spread that can mount nineteen men ain't to be overlooked in the betting."

"You think Telesco will know?"

"He'll damn well know we're up to something. Rittenhouse, when I found him in town, was in Frelton's place, glassy-eyed at a table with a couple of log rollers.

Telesco, apparently, had just hauled his freight. What I been getting at is no boss, regardless how spry he moves, can figure to be two places at once. Which means he's got to have help. Eyes in the back of his head, so to speak."

I gave this time to soak in, saw that even through the nervous shift of his stare, skinny Joe could find four as the sum of two twos. "I been sizing you up," I said to him, nodding. "From where I sit, you got the look of segundo. Think you can carry out orders? Give 'em to the rest of this outfit when I ain't around?"

His Adam's apple thumped like a boxful of hoppers. You could see the surprised satisfaction boil through him. His homely face turned solemn as a tenderfoot trapper with his hands full of skunk. It went without saying he would sure as hell try. Which was all you could reasonably ask of anyone.

"The job rates a raise," I told his embarrassment. "I'll see you get paid, including back wages . . . if I have to take it right out of my pocket."

Looked like I'd made a believer of him but I didn't let it get my hopes up too high. He was young and impressed but without much experience.

I chucked him a grin. Even a poor reed was better than none when a man was figuring to push through the tules. "Well," I said, "we might's well get at it."

The alert was out, no doubt about it.

Twice, as we worked our way between hills, motionless rifle packing horsebackers overlooked our approach from the distant ridges—inscrutably watching as we rode past. The boy's jumpiness increased. There was sweat on his lip as he jerked round to stare. Neither one of those watchers had the cut of herders or cowhands.

"What do you make of them?" I asked, to relax him.

"Hired guns," he said, scowling.

"It's plain you got a head on your shoulders. Ever see 'em before?"

"They didn't come with the place."

I told him: "You're learning."

"How we fixin' to keep the sheep out?—I mean, if they git past Turtle they'll be right onto us."

Turtle was Hardigan's outfit, bordering Boxed O to the north. "I don't expect," I said quietly, "they'll be coming that way."

"Then what would Rabas want with Boxed O?"

"Nuisance value. An ear to the ground if he can't use it otherwise. Probably reckoned, when he put up the money, to come in that way, but we've tromped on that notion. Size we are now—spread clean to hell and gone—he can't rely on those gunnies to open it up."

Joe peered at me, doubtful. Put the finger right on it. "You reckon to trust Hardigan?"

"With Rabas round the corner, I'm not about to trust anyone. If Lee's got the deck marked or thinks to deal from the bottom, he'll be in for a shock before he's many hours older."

Walking our horses round a bend in the gulch fetched the Boxed O headquarters damned near into our laps. "Appears we're expected. He's put a joker," I said, "in the cookshack with a carbine. Keep your lip buttoned but stand ready to back any play I make."

XV

Telesco was on the front porch in a rocker, trying to cling to a show of unconcern as false as the smile on a bartender's face. Both his bone handled pistols were strapped round his waist and the look he tipped up in pretended surprise couldn't quite hide the hate that burned back of his stare.

I pulled up near the steps, let Joe come alongside, and spent a few breaths just sitting there, quiet, giving our presence a chance to soak in.

When the thoughts squirming round in him got too wild to handle, the man growled in a rasping bluster, "What do you reckon you're doin', McGrath?"

"That any way to start off with a neighbor? Man might figure you got something around you don't want poked into. I didn't know better, I might think it was sheep."

Fright and fury flashed across those darkening cheeks but the surly glitter that came out of his stare wasn't the sort that precedes desperate action. He looked, mouth clamped, a sullen lump.

"Don't bother asking your guests to get down—I can say what I came to orate from the saddle. But before," I said, with a weighing glance, "we get down to brass tacks, you better know Joe here has orders—should your pal in the cookshack decide to take chips—to empty his shooter where it will do the most good."

Didn't seem to be necessary to ask if he'd got that. Telesco's cheeks were the color of damp wood ash.

"So just keep your paws on the arms of that rocker and do yourself a favor. Don't open your jaw till I've put you abreast of the new dispensation. That meeting last night was bad news for Rabas. Rocking Arrow picked up and will shortly absorb all the roundabout outfits, including Turtle and Debarra. I hope you can see what that does to your hand.

"There's no way he can reach you, hombre, without he crosses our land. If that doesn't bother you, maybe it should. We get any chatter from this neck of the woods, it'll be your last yell, and don't you forget it. Now get up off your ass!"

His eyes rolled like a stallion bronc's. A dry tongue rasped at drier lips and he seemed to shrink deeper into his clothes. Like an old lady crippled with rheumatism, he got onto his feet by cautious stages.

At the bend of the gulch, I let him get out from between our mounts.

"You done real well. But don't push your luck. Save some of that sweat for the day you decide crossing up Rabas is the worst of two choices. Take a page from the book of that tinhorn Frelton. A thought in time might save your life."

When we had got well away from the place, Joe let out his breath in a great whoosh of air. "Cripes a'mighty! I reckoned for a minute there you'd gone too far."

"You learn with his kind to keep up the pressure— it's when you ease off that you're up against trouble. We'll sift along now and have a few words with Hardigan."

He peered at me slanchways. After stewing in silence for a quarter of a mile he said, looking doubtful, "How much of a raise is this job goin' to get me?"

"Pace too hard on your arteries?"

"Don't you save up no fun for a rainy day?"

"There's generally enough to go round," I said.

"You got to do everything the hard way?"

"There's no easy way to get the hide off a polecat. The more time you give 'em, the smellier they get."

We went the rest of the way without conversation. When you break a man in to a new kind of work, it generally pays to hit the roughest chores first; he either stands up to those or you find someone else.

I wasn't too greatly concerned about Joe. He was

young and quick, not yet set in his ways. He would make me a hand or mighty soon I'd be shoveling dirt over him.

We found Hardigan at home, working over his books.

"Glad to see you're putting things in order," I said, when he mentioned this. "Guess your crew's not too pressed with chores that couldn't be saved for another day, are they?"

He was showing me a different facet of his nature. "What's on your mind?"

"Seems a good sort of day for a quick look around. Throw your kack on a horse and we'll go pick them up."

He studied me a moment with those cat's amber eyes. "All right," he nodded, and headed for the barn. Joe looked surprised. I chucked him a grin.

"How come he's bein' so goddam agreeable?"

"Curiosity, probably. He's nobody's fool."

The former owner of Turtle came out of the stable on a big rawboned stud horse that looked put together for considerable endurance. I didn't ask why he'd put his rig on a stallion. "You know where they're at, lead the way," I said quietly.

We found all three of them overhauling a windmill. If they were astonished to see Joe and me, they didn't show it. Hardigan called them down. "Catch up your horses," he said. "You're going with us."

I thought while his outfit was getting cinched up he might want to know what was next on the docket, but he kept his own counsel, leaving the play for me to put a name to. I expect he was some disappointed when this sly kind of bait was left plumb alone. I led off without comment, south by east in the direction that would keep us off Boxed O range. Telesco had enough to think about for the moment.

As we rode deeper into the rougher part of this terrain, onto range claimed by some of the smaller partners,

what cattle we saw were gaunt as snowbirds, piteousl
bawling. Hardigan gave these little notice, though hi
hands—in fairly strong language—made free to voic
their judgment of persons trying to ranch country tha
wouldn't support a family of jackrabbits.

First buildings we raised had more the look of som
squatter establishment than the headquarters layout
a cow operation. Bedeler, proprietor of this unlovely
collection, was reshaping iron on the flat of an anvil
no more apt at this than he was with the rest of his
endeavors apparently. He was big enough though t
hunt bears with a buggy whip. "You mind knocking off?"
I called, when he quit to peer at us, scowling.

"What fer?"

"Does it make any difference? Slap your hull on a
horse. We got riding to do."

"Don't let me keep you." He started pounding again.
Without further words I put a slug through his bel-
lows.

He came round with a yell but stayed in his tracks
when he saw where that gun snout was pointing. He
had a chaw in his cheek and said round the bulge of
it, "You got gall t' come over—"

"I've got other things, too, you won't like no better.
Paper you signed last night made this boar's nest part
of Rocking Arrow—"

"You fetch my share?"

"For Chrissake!" I said. "You'll get your shares from
the company lawyer."

Hefting his hammer, he growled looking up at me,
"That's when I'll put in that ridin'."

No one had to twist me around to be conscious of
Hardigan's sardonic amusement. You could feel the
piled-up weight of their stares, could see that what followed—like it or not—would be marking me long as I
stayed in this country, flavoring every order and action.

It wasn't just Joe I had to impress. I was bent over backward with talk already. If I couldn't handle this, I might's well fill in the hole and go home.

I came out of that saddle like hell wouldn't have me, ducked under his swing and cracked him across the face with my pistol. Steam I'd put into it slammed him, back-pedaling, fighting for balance.

He lost his hammer, banged into the anvil and hung there a moment, hulking and bloody with his eyes bulged enough to pop from their sockets and the flap of torn cheek dripping gore on his shirtfront.

More surprised than hurt, he shook his head like a bull and that gloved left hand, sent scrabbling behind him, came up with the smoking hot piece of bent iron as he lunged for me, snarling, the whole length of him triggered to beat my damn brains out.

It's instinctive, I guess, to throw out an arm when something comes at you. That's what I did with that iron whistling toward me—flung up my left arm and, nauseous with fury, felt the bone snap. Spun half around, I dived under the next and whacked my gun-barrel against his skull. He went down in a heap with a broken-off shout that would have curdled your sap to lay like Leviathan, eyes glazed and staring.

For a queasy breath-gagging moment, I reckoned I'd killed the muleheaded fool; the same thought looked from the shocked faces round me as they peered, pinched and gray, at the grotesque sprawl of that unwieldy huge shape.

Then he twitched and belched and a groan rolled out of him and the disgust in Hardigan's swiveling stare drove fresh life into my locked muscles. Bedeler, still groaning, got a knee levered under him and I rasped at Hardigan, "Help him up," and told one of the others, "Get a horse ready for him."

Joe, gray eyes still bright with excitement, growled,

"Better let me take a look at that arm." While he ginger-ly prodded and clucked, a pair of the others—with strips from his shirttail—bandaged Bedeler's torn cheek and head. "Can you work it?" Joe asked.

Though I nearly passed out, it seemed I was able to move the fingers some. With good right hand, I pushed the gun back in leather as Joe, looking hard at the sweat on my face, grumbled, "Little bone's broke. I better get you to town—"

"Tie it up."

Peering, uncertain, he finally shrugged and went off to find him a couple of boards, no great chore in a place like this where everything flapped to each lift of wind. While he worked, I busied myself with where that pair was ministering to Bedeler, watching that one of them didn't slip him a pistol. Way he was carrying on, you'd have thought he wasn't but half a step from the grave. When at last Joe said, "It'll have t' do," we got into our saddles.

Hardigan's eyes found mine. "Guess you'll be going to find you a doc—"

"We're going," I said, "where I set out to go," and told him to head for Rocking Arrow by whatever way was the next nearest outfit, another one-man spread the way it turned out, belonging to Gurley, the ex-San Saba livery barn keeper. Gurley took it in stride, offer-ing no objection to joining our party.

Though he kept his lip shut, I expect Kay's affianced found plenty of figuring to keep himself company. He must have been wondering what the hell I was up to, and the rest of them, too.

I kept my own counsel and wondered if my pain or Bedeler's was greatest. Certainly mine was all I could use and still stay in the saddle. Every jolt was like the twist of a knife but I roused myself when we came into the yard and saw Kay's stare, in the shade from the gallery, round and turn dark with an obvious concern.

It wasn't pity, I reckoned; certainly nothing personal. Just the compassion she'd feel for anything hurt. As a matter of fact, it was Bedeler's bandages that first caught her eye. It wasn't till—quitting the gallery—she'd come into the yard and was turning toward me for an explanation that she spotted the sling.

With her glance flitting over the roundabout faces, she came to a stop; her stare, troubled now, sought out the face she'd most naturally turn to. Getting out of the saddle, tossing Joe my reins, I could hear the anxious dread in her voice. "What is it? What's happened, Lee?"

And Hardigan's saturnine bark of a laugh. "Nothing any reasonable gent couldn't of avoided. Your friend there was showing how tough he could be."

XVI

Hanging onto my temper, I was turning away when this best of well wishers, calling after me, said: "With so much talk about sheep you think it's real smart to leave Turtle unguarded?"

"Joe," I said, "have Gurley and one of our boys ride over to keep an eye on the place."

Hardigan growled, "What's the matter with *my* hands?"

"As of last night you don't have any hands. Didn't you read that paper you signed?"

He had his mouth all puckered. But instead of the words he'd got loaded for me, he said, sounding close to the end of his patience, "All right—my *ex* hands. Any reason you can't send a couple of them back?"

"As it happens I've got other plans—"

"What are you trying to pull, McGrath?"

Kay put a hand on his arm. He shook loose of it. She said from an expressionless face: "Let it go, Lee," but there was enough of an edge to her tone to get through to him.

You could see just the same that he was still of two minds, brows pulled down in the lowering scowl twisting the thin mouth below that big nose. "This feller ain't Gawd A'mighty!"

I showed them how patient a man could be. "Doesn't it make sense I'd think first of Rocking Arrow, putting the convenience of individuals later?

"Most of you people I don't know from Adam. In any carload lot there are generally mavericks that figure personal profit above the good of their partners. Since I don't have the time to sort wheat from chaff, the surest insurance I've been able to come up with is to shift folks around. And this I will do no matter who doesn't like it." Then I said, not much caring: "Aren't you a *reasonable* man, Mister Hardigan?"

You could almost hear him grinding his teeth. He wasn't scarcely a breath from busting his surcingle when Kay Wilbur said in a tone coolly level, "I'll see you in my office, McGrath. Inside the next half hour."

Hardigan's horse was gone when I went over.

Kay Wilbur came at once to the point. "Why do you keep pushing him, McGrath?"

"I'm not pushing him, ma'am."

"You know what I mean." Below that red hair, her green eyes swept my face with the kind of impatience you can expect from a woman dealing as an owner with a tiresome hired hand. "You surely can't imagine he'd sell out Rocking Arrow. Why do you two keep riding each other?"

"Hard to say, ma'am. Guess at heart we're just a couple stray dogs growling over a bone."

I could feel the weight of those searching eyes. "What bone?"

"Why . . . this outfit, I suppose—what else? Guess it's natural he should take a pretty considerable interest."

Deepening color stained the center of each cheek but she said, still with that weighing look to her stare, "Wouldn't it be just as natural for you—as a range boss hoping to stay on—to play up to him? At least make some effort to keep on his good side?"

"You could put it that way. Happens I don't have to trim sail or depend on his favor to stay in this job."

"Really?" she said. "And how did you reach that interesting conclusion?"

I could tell by the thinning line of her lips I was piling black marks up like jots in a tally book. "Guess you and friend Hardigan found more agreeable things to take up your time than any clause by clause look at that agreement you signed."

"What's that supposed to mean?"

"Means I can't be sent packing except by majority vote of all shareholders."

She looked kind of startled. "I did notice something about a vote . . . but I thought it referred to those holding stock in—"

"Yes, ma'am. That's right. Conrado can tell you I paid him cash money for five shares of this outfit."

Swift changes of thought chased themselves through her stare while she was trying to cover up how this bit of news hit her. "I didn't suppose you had any money."

"Bribes often take that shape," I said shortly, and something passed over her cheeks like doubt before she clamped lips with a lift of the chin. "I wouldn't have thought—" But she quit that line, too, to say coldly hard as the whip of a well chain, "You're not much for pretty are you, McGrath?"

I could feel the heat coming up through my collar. Not all she stirred in me stemmed from the nag of that broken bone when I growled, "Prettiness, ma'am, is no crutch against sheep."

"I guess you're right about that. When you go in to have your arm looked at, perhaps you had better have a word with that woman at the Buffalo Bull—Mrs. Frelton, is it? She was out here this morning. Seemed rather upset when I said you were gone."

"I'm not the marrying kind," I said, hitting back where I could. "But I'll have the doc take a whack at the arm. The crew while I'm gone will take orders from Joe."

Not caring to listen to her views on that, I wheeled toward the pens with a jerk of the head to find Joe approaching with a fresh saddled horse. I took the reins he held out and said loud enough for her to hear my instructions: "You're in charge till I get back. See that you keep your eyes peeled sharp and don't let Bedeler out of your sight."

It was full dark with a lift of wind coming off the flats when I picked up the lights of Bad News an hour later. They weren't many nor bright, most of this shine coming out of the Bull. The store, oddly enough, was completely dark. Two-three distant lamps dimly glimpsed through the dark only served to point up the town's cutoff character and deepen the isolated loneliness of it.

I rode on up the street, past the front of Frelton's place, covertly inspecting the lone horse tied there, unable in this way to make out its brand or even to be certain it was not a local mount. Always there in my mind, never far from the surface, was the knowledge that one day my past would catch up in the shape of some stranger packing a badge.

Turning in at the first lighted shack, I got awkwardly

down to climb the three steps and pound on the door. This didn't seem to be followed by any noticeable activity. But just as I was lifting my hand to try again, the door was pulled open to frame a tousle-haired man in braces and shirtsleeves standing barefooted against that far light.

"Yes?"

"Can you tell me where I can locate the Doc?"

"Jabbart?"

"We blessed with two?"

He rubbed at a scratchy cheek. "Not that I've heard," he finally grunted, and stepped somewhat relucantly out of the way. "I'm Jabbart—come in."

I got a whiff of his breath as I went past and understood better the time it had taken him to get to the door. I guessed we all had our problems, though it struck me as odd how many of the West's bone-setters and pill-rollers turned out in my experience to be solitary drinkers.

"Sit down," he said from beside a white painted table, and turned up the lamp.

After cutting Joe's sling and board pieces off me and gingerly inspecting the discolored tight skin of that swollen lower arm, he clucked a couple times, poured himself another slug and, eyeing me slanchways, wanted to know when the injury had occurred. Also what had caused it.

"A length of iron bar. This morning."

He carefully felt the arm again. "This will hurt," he said, squeezing.

I damn near went through the top of my skull when the bone ends grated together. He considered my sweat and shoved a look at the bottle. "You want a jolt of that stuff?"

"Not unless you're figuring to do that again."

Blowing out his cheeks he got a pair of thin splints

from a shelf against the wall, put a couple turns of gauze around the arm where pain was greatest and bound the splints in place. He went to the sink, half filled a pan with water, dug out a jar of white powder and was fetching these back to the table when I said, "Never mind the plaster."

He regarded me from under raised, tufted brows. "That's not going to mend overnight you know. If it slips out of place—"

"How much do I owe you?"

He fixed me a sling with an old maid's fussiness. "Couple bucks," he said, and I paid him.

XVII

Back on the horse, I sat a while considering the lights of the Buffalo Bull and what Kay had said about Frelton's widow . . . the buxom Angie with the spun gold hair. I could tell myself she had nothing I wanted, but that ride she had made to Rocking Arrow this morning and her upset condition at finding me gone, if Kay hadn't just plain made that up, suggested this conclusion might not cover all the facts.

She might be what she looked, just another cheap trollop, determined to leave no stone unturned which might cause me to reconsider her proposition. She could have come onto information vital to my welfare, or be simply laying pipe to get even for that turndown. A woman scorned—particularly one in her situation—didn't hold out much I cared to get mixed up with.

I remembered her bawling in that hotel room. I reminded myself that—through Frelton at least—she'd some kind of connection with Rabas' man Telesco—and I remembered Telesco, only this morning in that little chat we'd had, using my name as though he knew more about me than circumstances warranted.

Sure I'd told him my name. Right in front of the Bull just after I'd tied into him that day over Kay. But it hadn't seemed to mean a thing to him them.

Someone, apparently, had wised him up since. With those woodchoppers' help, he'd got it out of Rittenhouse about that meeting I'd set up at Rocking Arrow. According to Angie, he'd cleared out of her place in considerable of a hurry, as though almost he'd rushed off to spread the news. And, although she hadn't said this in so many words, she had certainly implied he had an interest in the Bull. I had the feeling, moreover, Frelton's woman was afraid of him—why else would she be trying to hire me?

Deep in my bones I reckoned it smart to stay away from that place, but her acquaintance with Telesco drew me Bullward like a magnet.

Loosening the pistol in my holster, I nudged the horse into motion. This probably wasn't the brightest thing I'd ever done but if she'd found out something she'd thought important enough to take that long ride out to the ranch, I'd be a fool indeed to have come this near and go riding off without affording her a chance to speak.

The closer I got, the more it smelled like a trap.

A man doesn't ride cheek by jowl with peril for as long as I'd been, without developing a kind of sixth sense. A hundred yards from the front of the place, I paused in a deeper smudge of shadows to consider my situation again.

Nothing moved in my sight. No sound came out of those weaving dapples the lamps of the Bull cast through wind-tossed branches—but this, of course, could be natural enough with that horse gone now from where it had been tied.

Yet real as the touch of a probing hand I could feel in the hairs at the back of my neck the creep and proximity of imminent danger. Where had the crickets gone? Where . . . and why?

Easing out of the saddle, I left the horse hitched to a scruffy bush and—instead of approaching the slats of its batwings—worked around through the dark to come up on its side. And found no windows. Straining my ears did me no good, either.

On the balls of my feet, I slipped along toward the rear. Rounded the corner and, careful of trash, guided by a thin sliver of light inched my way toward a door that, oddly enough, had been left off the latch.

You bet I had plenty of jabs about that.

Just out of spitting distance from this invitation I stood with cold flesh rippling over my spine and for perhaps half a dozen thumps of my heart considered that motionless left-ajar door.

I could back off a bit, wait and see what developed. But playing this safe was an old woman's game holding little appeal to a man in my boots who, by stepping inside with a gun-weighted fist, could find out in two shakes what this score added up to.

Sure I knew this could be—if a trap had been baited—exactly what the baiter intended. It wasn't too likely that thin slice of door had been left unlatched through somebody's carelessness. On the other hand, though, who had reason to imagine Kay's ramrod would show up in town at this time of night? This town? This night?

Angie Frelton perhaps. And her partner, Telesco?

There was one sure way to find out, and I took it.

With the solid assurance of a Colt's .45 lifted ready to throw down if I was stepping into something to be settled no other way, nagged by the throb of that broken bone, I looked harder at the door, wondering if touching it would loose a warning skreak.

I moved three cautious steps and with the pistol's muzzle set against it, gently pushed.

It gave no racket. Only the draft of its opening touched me. When the space was big enough, I slipped through to find myself in a cubbyhole room stacked with barrels and kegs and a doorless arch ten feet ahead that showed me a section of the bar's back side with two shelves of bottles and the stock of what was probably a sawed-off shotgun. *The Greener Angie'd held the last time I'd been in there?*

The only sound was the ticking of a clock. None of the normal noises habitually heard in this kind of place. No conversations. No throats being cleared—not even, by God, the rasp of a curse.

Was the place empty then? If so, where was Angie?

Would she have gone somewhere without locking up? With the lamps all lit and whisky there for the taking?

I would get no forwarder, mouth open, standing here.

Dropping into a crouch, I slammed the door shut behind me.

In the barroom somebody swore. *"What was that?"*

Angie said, "Goddam latch!"

"What latch?"

"Storeoom door. Wind's blown it shut. I been after Frelton to get the thing fixed, but you know how he was."

The strange voice said: "You tell me."

"Shiftless."

"That's right." Telesco laughed. "Never was a hand to do anything today he could shift—"

The same heavy voice growled, "Quit the yammerin'." Boots moved across the barroom floor. A man's head and shoulders came into my vision across the top of the bar. A scraggle of beard and a hard burnt face with a low-crowned, sweat-darkened Texas hat pulled down across eyes that showed red rimmed and lashless as the thick neck twisted a look toward the arch.

I dropped onto my footheels in the heavier shadow cast by the bar. Something about that thin-mouthed face with its tawny moustache seemed to tug at my memory though I felt reasonably sure I'd never seen him before. I heard the ching of his spurs and increased impatience growl through the tone that told one of the others to go take a look.

"My feet hurt," Angie whined, begging off.

"Oh, fer Chrissake," Telesco snarled, starting forward. "She already told you. It's only the wind—"

"Bolt the damn thing then!"

Covered by the sounds Telesco made coming toward me I pushed the .45 into my waistband and duck-waddled forward in a grab for the Greener. I got hold of it right enough, had it off the shelf and was thumbing back the hammers when a gasp jerked my head up to find Angie staring down at me.

With no opportunity to gauge intentions, I emptied both barrels through the front of that bar.

XVIII

It made a terrible racket.

If the amount of damage proved in any way comparable, there was no call for hurry about exposing myself. Through the splintery hole in that near black mahogany, I could see a trousered leg and it was not putting weight on the boot that came out of it.

The tinkle of broken glass was still filtering from the echoes when I caught the pound of a running horse and, remembering Frelton's woman, let go of the shotgun to snatch up my pistol and duck back away from her as I shoved to my feet.

She looked anything but warlike with her mouth gaping open and her eyes large as egg cups in the pinched and frozen pallor of that shocked and painted face.

"Jesus Christ! Did you have to ruin my goddam bar?"

I backed out from behind it with my mind on that leg and found Telesco, as expected, stretched prone on the floor. From the blood soaking through the ripped tatters of vest, I didn't see much chance of him ever again bothering anyone.

With the diminishing hoof sound of the recent departure fading into obscurity, there seemed little point in doing much hunting for the heavy-voiced hombre who'd been dishing out the orders.

Angie was still angrily eyeing her bar. "Who," I said, "was the one that got away?"

Her stare filled with outrage. "Why, for Pete's sake, couldn't you have been home when I rode way to hell an' gone out there to tell you!"

"Tell me what?"

"About *him!* Yesterday he was round here all afternoon and half the night askin' questions! You'd of thought he was fixin' to put your name in his will—"

"All I want is his handle."

"Charlie Ostermann."

I nodded. "Rabas' right hand." It figured. "What kind of spurs was he wearing?"

"Spurs?"

"Them things a man puts on his boots to make the horse go."

She looked at me oddly. "What difference does that make?" She didn't seem to care for what she read in my face and backed away a couple of steps. "Look—it wasn't my fault them two was camped in this place! How was I to know they was having me watched? They was in here waitin' when I got back from Rocking Arrow . . . one of Telesco's hands come in right behind

me and told the pair of them where I'd been. Then
Telesco said if Ostermann wanted to look at you—"

"Gold or silver?" I threw at her bleakly.

"It's kind of odd you should ask that." She swallowed
uncomfortably. "Now don't get your mad up—I'm tellin'
you, ain't I? First time I saw him he had gold ones on
but when he come in yesterday—"

"He was wearing the same kind as everybody else,"
I said, thinly grinning, seeing a number of things now
which had escaped me before. "You had a right to be
scared." Because it wasn't Telesco that had been Frelton's partner—*her* partner now. It was Gold Spur Charlie, the studhorse gun boss of Rabas' fighting sheepmen
that had turned her mind to getting hold of my talent.
Gold Spur Charlie, who had but one use for women
and cared not a bit whose women he used.

"You ain't goin' to leave him there like that, are you?"
she cried at me shrilly as I moved toward the batwings.
I shoved on through and turned up the road and
found my horse and got into the saddle, mind back in
Texas going over the black burnt-into-me things which
had led me to kill that San Saba banker . . . mainly—
as I saw these things now—because I couldn't find
Charlie and had discovered it was the bank's man who
had set the whole bastardly sequence in motion. He
had probably never imagined events would take the
turn they had but he had pointed Charlie at her and
since I'd had to strike out at something, he'd become
the handiest target.

Looking back never buttered no parsnips and I
pulled my mind away from it. But thoughts have a life
of their own I'd found and mine stayed deep in that
dark bitter spiral that had taken me finally to the rocks
of a chain gang, inexorably following every step of the
way.

The Providence which looks after fools and drunks must have been watching over me with loving care or I would never have gotten back to Rocking Arrow alive.

I was paying no attention to where the horse took me, when a blue whistler dropped him, spilling me into the trailside rocks while the unseen rifleman emptied his magazine.

Charlie, of course. Too cagey to check up.

I heard the son of a bitch ride off before the far rumbling of echoes had even died out in the roundabout hills. Damn little use going after him without a mount, but one thing I knew—he would never get that good a chance again.

The night sky was graying when I turned into the Wilbur yard. I'd left the saddle but not my rifle. Still lugging it, I went into the snoring sounds of the bunkhouse. They were all sawing wood so I stretched myself dog-wearily out on the first vacant bed I came to, divested of nothing but my boots and hat. It occurred to me later what a fool thing that was, with the shack being shared by the greasysacker, Bedeler. But the saint who had saved me from Charlie's rifle must have been looking after me still I suppose.

It was mid afternoon and hotter than the hinges when I woke up in the emptied shack. My bones felt like they'd been run through a gristmill and the taste of my mouth was brassy with bile. Too much sleep always leaves me groggy but presently I got the hat on my head, stomped into my boots and went across to the cookshack where Rittenhouse was skinning the jackets off a lapful of spuds. "I suppose," he grumbled, looking up with a scowl, "I got to quit what I'm doin' an' fix you a meal."

"Coffee and whatever's handy will do."

"It had better," he said, and chopped some spuds in a skillet with some leftover beans and a chunk of fat sowbelly which he took outside to put on the Dutch oven.

"Where's Bedeler?" I said, sitting down on a bench.

"Gone off with the crew on orders from that kid. Claims you've made him some kind of straw boss. If that's the best you could do, this spread is sure in for—"

"Where's Hardigan?"

"Allowed he had to go home about somethin'. You think *he'd* take orders from the likes of Joe?"

I might imprudently have answered that if I hadn't caught sight of the way he was eyeing me. If Turtle's ex-owner had set this up as some kind of test—perhaps of my authority—I would have to find some way of bringing him to heel. Give a man like him half an inch and you'd have more trouble than I'd had with Bedeler. Just thinking of the man made my arm ache worse, and I turned my thoughts again to Charlie for distraction.

It seemed plain to me now where that message about his demise had been sprung from. Almost certainly Shannon's doing.

He'd probably reckoned—and rightly—I would be more easily put into the role he wanted me to play, if I were suddenly made to think Charlie was dead.

A stopgap strategy if ever I'd seen one. It had worked—that was the main thing, and possibly all he cared about. It had slickly put me where I was; and he'd figured, no doubt, on events—plus that rockpile—keeping my shoulder shoved to the wheel. But he didn't know what I had against Ostermann.

Or did he? How hard had he dug to find out about me? Given his incentive, he may well have suspected there'd be a woman at the bottom of it *even if he hadn't found out which woman.* Maybe he'd reckoned by the time I discovered the skunk I'd been hunting was still in the quick, I would be too involved to pull out of this deal.

There was no way to know and I didn't much care. He would probably be just as well suited if I *did* kill Charlie. What the major wanted was a full-scale blood bath, enough gore splashed around that that bunch back at Washington couldn't avoid realizing the need for controls.

I pushed back my plate and stood away from the table.

Hoof sound was shuffling through the open door and windows and I could see a brace of riders entering the yard. "There's Bedeler now," Rittenhouse grunted. But it wasn't Bedeler that had my attention. I had told Joe distinctly not to let the greasysacker out of his sight. And it wasn't Joe with him. It was that double damned Hardigan.

XIX

Reminding myself that he was, after all, Kay Wilbur's chosen, I stepped through the door and tight-lipped, waited for the pair to approach.

But the smug sort of grin that was twisting Hardigan's mouth as he watched me undid considerable of my better intentions. The gall of the man taking off like he had and now coming back in the company of Bedeler furnished no oil against the heat of my temper.

They were bound for the pens to put up their horses when my hail turned them toward me. Hardigan said something under his breath that put a like glint into Bedeler's stare. "What," I said, when the two of them pulled up, "do you rannies find so amusing?" And, when this got me nothing but more of the same, to Bedeler I said: "Joe run out of work for you?"

As though she had been on the lookout for him, Kay chose that moment to appear on the gallery, calling Hardigan's name. He chucked her a casual wave without ever taking his eyes from my face. His grin, if anything, looked to become even broader, as though my stare or my words gave added glee to whatever hugged secret they were sharing between them.

"I asked you, Bedeler, a reasonable question."

Behind the flattening twist of his mouth, the greasy-sacker answered with a kind of studied insolence, "I ain't been feelin' too good. If you got to know, he sent Lee along to make sure I got back here."

He had a strip of court plaster stuck across his ripped cheek and his hat pulled over the left side of his head to make space for the bandage where my pistol had struck him.

"We've got no room on this spread for sick chickens," I told him. "Grab a shovel and a barrow and clean out those corrals."

I saw the glance he flung Hardigan. The big-nosed man said, "Better get at it. You heard the boss."

I took a hitch on my temper as Bedeler turned reluctantly away.

"Lee—" Kay Wilbur called from the gallery.

"Just a minute," I said, as he reached for his reins. "I'd like to know how come Joe sent you back with him."

"You heard the man, didn't you?"

"I'm not one to believe everything I hear."

"Don't push so hard," he said from darkening cheeks. And, in a more guarded tone: "Five shares of Rocking Arrow ain't much protection against a bullet."

With a short ugly laugh he turned his mount toward where Kay waited.

I wanted mightily to wipe that sneer off his face but this was hardly the time or cause for that sort of showdown. It occurred to me also that a man who had moved from procrastinations to threats must have found some new confidence to bolster his nerve, and I could not help wondering if this twisty whelp had gone whole hog and—despite the desperate straits Rabas and the sheep crowd had put this Basin's ranchers in—sent off a tip to some Texas marshal or had got in touch maybe with the prison authorities who'd been hunting high and low to get their hands on me again.

Wherever he'd dug up this new found bravado, there wasn't much I could do to offset it at the moment without inviting gunplay. I wasn't all that sure the contract drawn up for this deal by the courtly Conrado could stand up to such pressure. If it came down to a vote, as things stood right now, the girl would probably have me out of here.

I watched Bedeler pull the rig off his horse and turn the tired animal into the day pen. I saw Hardigan go into the house with Kay Wilbur and then watched Bedeler limp off toward the bunkhouse. Just as I was about to lift my voice at him, the scissorsbill, putting on the look of a martyr, swung off to the left in the direction of the barn to roust out the barrow and shovel I had ordered.

Keeping the sheep out of this Four Peaks country was—presumably—one of the chores Shannon had in mind when, back at Sunflower, he'd hornswoggled me into this deal. Not the main one, perhaps, but keeping Rabas out wasn't like to be accomplished without a lot of blood being spilled along the way.

Yet I didn't see how I could very well hang and rattle here at Rocking Arrow if Hardigan had put the law on my trail . . . unless, of course, the major—foreseeing some such contingency—had taken steps to circumvent this. And the more I pushed this around in my head, the more reasonable it seemed he very probably had.

Just as obviously, I—Pete McGrath—would be the last one to know.

But this notion did put more spring in my step as, observing Bedeler heading for the corrals with the tools I'd called for, I trailed along after him and, preempting a seat on one of the top poles, prepared to make sure he did the job right.

I tried to think what other steps I might be taking to make sure friend Rabas bit off more than he could chew. One move did occur to me which, besides advantages at once apparent, might gall Mr. Hardigan almost as much as it'd infuriate Rabas.

With this in mind, I kept one eye on Hardigan's horse and when at last he stepped out to get onto it, I got off my perch and beckoned him over.

It was plain he didn't much like this and equally plain he was minded to disregard a summons not put in the form of an order; so I made up his mind by calling him over.

He drew rein with a look that might permanently have blighted any growth less resistant than an ironwood shoot. "What now?" he growled, blowing out his cheeks as though he had run half across the yard to get here.

"Thought you might know what that sheep crowd paid to get hold of Boxed O."

Obviously puzzled and patently hunting for what I was getting at, he peered at me harder. With all expression ironed from his cheeks, "Why should I?" he countered.

"Had the idea it might be common knowledge."

It evidently was. "Two thousand," he grumbled.

"Seems kind of high for what they got for their money."

"It ain't everyone would have the damn guts to sell out his neighbors to a puke like Telesco."

"I'm glad to heard you say that," I nodded. "And I expect in your turn you will be some tickled to hear I'm taking over that spread."

His jaw got away from him. Fighting astonishment, Hardigan was unable to keep the bulge from his stare. "It surprises you?" I said.

He got hold of himself, the look on his face changing into a sneer. "You'll find that easier said than accomplished."

"Get your horse," I said. "We'll soon find out."

His jaw slumped again. "You gone clean off your rocker?"

"If you're that afraid, I'll take cook along." I yelled Rittenhouse's name and when his head showed in the cookshack door, "Catch up your horse and saddle one for me."

"Hell," Hardigan snarled, "I've as much guts as *you* have!"

"Fine," I said, "we'll all three of us go."

After stewing in silence the longest half of the way, Hardigan, swearing in exasperation, cried, "We ought, by Gawd, to have our heads looked at!"

I said blandly: "Something bothering you?"

"You can't buffalo that feller!" He looked pretty steamed up. "If you're right about him workin' for Rabas, you ought to know *that* without my tellin' you!"

"Telesco and Rabas aren't the same breed of cats. Telesco's nothing but a pistol packing polecat. Thing he uses for a thinkbox ain't hardly bigger than you could find on a gopher."

Hardigan glared. "If he's that dumb, he's going to

grab for his cutter and this brainwave of yours'll wind up in a shoot-out!"

"You can wait right here if it will make you feel safer."

XX

Looked like for a moment I had pushed him too far.

His ruddy flushed-up face turned dark and then livid with a fury too fierce, it appeared, for the tie ropes of his restraints to control. A big fist slammed toward the sag of his holster while in plain view of coosie I locked both hands round the horn of my saddle.

Hard to say if this stopped him. But though he left the gun where it was, the will to murder stared naked and quivering from those ginger-colored eyes.

Next time, I thought, his hatred of me might very well drive him hell-bent to a showdown, and what was I going to say to Kay Wilbur then?

"If it will ease your mind any," I said to him quietly, "Telesco is dead and, by this time, probably planted."

It was plain he didn't know whether to believe me or not—couldn't seem to decide even whether he wanted to. So I helped him along. "Appears he caught up with a bad case of lead poisoning."

Hardigan's eyes winnowed down to slits. "You killed him!"

"I didn't have much choice. While you and me was pasearing round yesterday, Frelton's widow rode out to the ranch. Seems she was upset when told I wasn't there. So after the doc got through with me last night, I stepped over to the Bull to find out what she wanted. Telesco and Ostermann were camped out there waiting. They'd had the widow followed and—toting up what things they could put together—came up with the notion this was just too good a chance to let pass."

"What happened to Ostermann?"

"Expect he had to see a man about a dog."

Kay Wilbur's affinity looked about as comfortable as a motherless calf. He didn't seem so much riled now as rightdown nervous. The way his eyes flipped around you might think he was expecting Rabas' right bower to come flying in on the wings of a dove. "Don't you realize," he said hoarsely, "he may be out there now, holed up at Boxed O with Telesco's crew—"

"I certainly hope so. If we could take him out along with Telesco, we'd have his boss pretty much over a barrel. We couldn't be so lucky," I said to him dryly, heeling my horse into motion again, not honestly caring if he strung along or not.

Rittenhouse—coosie—said out of a considerable silence: "I'm glad that son of a bitch is dead!"

Hardigan flipped a sullen look at him and the cook sank back into closed-faced communion with whatever satisfactions his own thoughts afforded.

Up till now, anyway, I hadn't uncovered any sign of pickets. If that pair which had watched Joe and me ride in were anywhere around, they were being extra careful to keep out of our sight.

This hardly made much sense unless they'd set up an ambush, which—to me—did not appear either reasonable or likely. When you chop off a snake's head there's almost sure to be some wriggling but I've yet to find one trying to get back at me.

We rode into the gulch giving onto Boxed O, coosie still entranced with the pictures in his head, Hardigan scowling with his eyes flapping round like a bunch of bullbats out hunting their suppers. I expect he considered me just about ripe for a string of spools, but I wasn't as reckless as I probably looked. If I didn't draw rein coming up on that bend it was mostly because I didn't want to get there and finds the birds flown.

What cattle we saw was so puny and gaunted they looked like they hadn't got more than one gut.

Our first sight of the layout, from the evidence in hand, gave ample indication whoever was inside had not been figuring to tarry overlong. A pair of tail switching horses stood on dropped reins just outside the porch, warsacks strapped behind their saddles.

Rittenhouse asked: "We gonna make good Injuns outa these whippoorwills?" and hauled the Winchester from under his knee.

"Only if they run," I said, "or dig for their hardware."

Hardigan, clamp-jawed, rifle across kness, nudged his mount to the left while coosie opened up a like space off my right. We were half across the weed-grown yard when the door, flung open, disgorged a pair of whiskered hardcases, each with arms wrapped about a load of plunder.

The bigger gent was stepping off the porch when the man behind him let out a yell.

"Hold it right there," I said, and all motion stopped.

Behind the bulge of shocked-wide stares I could read the thoughts wheeling through their skulls. "Take a good tight hold—drop that stuff and you're in line for a harp. Where's the rest of this outfit?"

"Left right after the word got around."

It was the lanky one answered and had the look of begrudging the vanished men's foresight. I grinned at him sourly. "You fellers crippled?"

The beanpole glared. He growled in a blustery tone of defiance, "We had wages comin'—"

"Reckon you've picked up enough to make up for it?"

The spokesman appeared to have got talked out. I said to the squatty one: "You can do better than that,"

THE TEXAS GUN

and dug the money belt from under my shirt. "Didn't
I hear you say this place was for sale?"

The loudmouthed one goggled but this paisano was
quick to catch on. Distrustful, but greedy, he jerked
his face in a nod. "Expect you did—but it's cash on
the barrelhead." Grinning, he said, "We ain't fixed to
give credit."

"Pretty rundown," I told him, "but I'll give what
was paid for it and trust you to pass it along to Rabas."

This would take most of my roll but looked to be
worth it, in satisfaction anyway. I considered the pair
of them. A pretty sorry lot; the one who'd first spotted
us being sawed-off so short he'd have had to borrow a
ladder to kick a gnat on the ankle.

To this one I said, "You can put down your keep-
sakes. I'm handing you, for whoever bought in here, fifteen hundred U.S. dollars, no strings attached. Only
thing I want in exchange is a receipt signed by both
of you acknowledging I put the money in your hands.
You got something I can write on?"

Shorty dropped his plunder and dug out a tally book,
found a blank page and handed it up to me with a
stub of pencil he fished from his hatband.

No matter how carefully worded this could be shown
in court to be pretty high-handed but I didn't really
reckon it would ever get that far. Some things a man
likes to collect for in person and I figured friend Rabas
for one of that kind.

"Just a simple and ordinary bill of sale," I said, handing it back with book and pencil. "Both you gents put
your John Henrys on it just under where it says 're-
ceived from P. McGrath cash money in the amount of
fifteen hundred dollars.' Case your eyesight's bad, you
can put your monickers—as they appear on the payroll
—right after them exes.

"That's fine," I said, taking the paper back and handing over the money. "I'll put the date on this now and these boys can sign as witnesses. Case you've got a train to catch or something, you're free to take off. Any time you're a mind to— Something fretting *you?*"

The big one said, peering hard at me, "How far do we get before you bucks start shootin'?"

"If you behave, there won't no one get shot. Go on. Climb on those horses and pull your freight. Just make sure you keep riding."

Before the pair had even got out of sight, Hardigan growled like there was nothing under my hat but hair: "That sheepherder's got about half as much chance ever seein' that money as a wax cat tourin' hell with the blower on!"

"Them boys sure looked plenty greedy, didn't they?"

Hardigan's jaw hung down like a hoofshaper's apron. "Helll!" he snorted, and dug for more breath. "That's the looniest deal I ever met up with! Not if he lives to be older than Christ is that range grabbin' buck gonna give up this—"

"He's already give it up. I've got a recept signed by—"

"He won't know 'em from—"

"He can't get around their names in the paybook. He can't prove I didn't buy this place in good faith."

Hardigan gave me a pitying look.

"You're forgetting one thing," I said. "I've got possession."

I reckon he figured all I knew about brains was you could buy them with scrambled eggs at a hash house. He grabbed for more air with kind of a snarl. "You don't think he's gonna *leave* it like that?"

"How well do you know him?" I said to Hardigan's glare.

"I don't *have* to know him to know *goddam well*

he'll come swarmin' in here like hell wouldn't have him!
You tryin' to get us all killed?"

I said, kind of grinning, "Maybe you'd like to sell
out to me, too?"

He didn't think that was funny. Before he could
work up his steam again, I said to the cook, handing
over my paper, "I want you to hit out for Sunflower
pronto. Tell Conrado to put this where it's not like to
be lost, get the sale recorded and see that change of
ownership is put on record at the assessor's office. He's
to make sure, you tell him, Rabas gets wind of—"

"He *can't* record it," Hardigan cut in, "without he
can show a deed to the place or money in escrow."

"What do you suppose we hired the man for?"

"*We* didn't hire him," Hardigan growled. "An' if you
figure to drag Rockin' Arrow into this—"

"I may look a prize boob but when I pay for something right out of my pocket you can bet your boots I'll
get put down as owner. Go on," I said to Rittenhouse,
"hit a lope. And while you're over there, find out if
he's heard anything from that wire."

XXI

I can't say what change came over Hardigan—I was
watching the cook. "Wire?" he said, with surprise in
his stare.

"Nothing wrong with your hearing. If it's come, fetch
it back with you." I waved him away.

As might have been expected, Hardigan's cheeks were
awash with suspicion. "*What* wire?"

"Wire," I said, "to fence Rabas out."

He cried like a man on the verge of apoplexy: "You
think a few strands of wire'll stop *him?* Why, it would

cost a fortune and he'd just rip it out! Who's going to pay for it?" he shouted, red all the way to his collar line.

"We're only putting up fence where it will do the most good. I don't expect it to stop him—he won't be stopped till somebody puts a lead plum through his skull. But, along with a few other things I've thought up, it should slow him down enough—mad as the loss of this spread's going to make him—that most of the corpses should come off his side of the ledger."

The former Turtle boss banged shut his jaws with a clack that must have been hard on his molars, and the eyes glaring out of that puckered-up face held a rage incompatible with anything I'd said. It could have been, I suppose, the visible effect of all the points we disagreed on, or it may have been related to the things he'd hoped to attain by marrying Kay Wilbur.

It could have been no more than the clash of personalities.

Deep in my bones it made me wonder if he'd closer ties with the man under discussion that would seem on the surface to be wholly feasible.

I couldn't see how this made much sense unless—by some arrangement long ago arrived at—his spread and Kay's had been set up to be exempt from whatever Rabas intended with regard to this area.

When he got enough hold on himself, what finally came hoarsely out of him was: "Is a gun your answer to *everything*, McGrath?"

"Sometimes," I said, "I find a knife more convenient."

He continued to stare at me unpleasantly. "There are ways of putting a stop to your high-handedness—"

"I expect you've explored most of those already." Fed up with his gab I told him, "When we get back to headquarters you can have a go at Miss Wilbur. Maybe she'll think of something you've overlooked."

Riding into the Rocking Arrow yard, I said to him, "We may as well get to the bottom of this. We'll get the gear off these horses and I'll step over there with you."

He didn't say anything but reined his mount toward the house, blackly scowling. I rode on to the corrals and took care of my own horse. Bedeler, I noted, had cleaned the pens, put up the barrow and tucked himself out of sight. I thought straight off he had probably cleared out, but a quick look around proved he hadn't gone that far. His horse was still here.

I went over to the bunkhouse and found him there, stretched out in the heat with nothing on but his underwear. "Until further notice, you'll cook for this outfit. Go wash yourself up and get at it," I said.

Ignoring his glower, I went back outside and headed for the house, knowing what I had in mind would not improve my popularity. The dull ache of my arm didn't much relieve my outlook, either. But time was running out on this deal and without we moved quick we could find Rabas onto us before I was set to deal with his Yaquis.

I hadn't forgot about Ostermann. I didn't reckon he had gone to ground since I'd seen him last night at the Buffalo Bull. After knocking that horse out from under me, I didn't really look to see him again romping around this range until he had enough help to feel sure he could bury me.

The angry growl of Hardigan's voice chopped off when they heard my boots cross the gallery. "Come in, McGrath," Kay called to my knock.

Pulling open the screen, I went along to the office, finding her chosen with one hip on the desk like he reckoned that much of it belonged to him anyway. The eyes looking out of him were like burning coals.

"You've heard his views about the wire—"

"I'm a lot more interested," she said sober faced, "in this swindle you've set up to play on that sheep crowd. That's a heap more money than I would be willing to pour down that particular kind of a rat hole. Puts a pretty stiff price on those Rocking Arrow shares you weaned from Conrado—"

"Not weaned, ma'am. Those were bought with cash right out of my pocket. And what I paid for Boxed O hasn't anything to do with them."

I could feel the hard edge of her stare digging into me. "What *did* you expect to get for the money you so gratuitously handed that pair of—"

"A double barreled bargain. As you've probably just had pointed out to you, I got rid of two gun hands— which I call a bonus in anybody's language. I got possession of a ranch which must have figured pretty prominent in Rabas' plans and, by that token, put a burr under his saddle that's like to gall him considerable."

"You seem to have a talent for galling other people."

"Most of them, I find, if you get them mad enough, tend to jump without half looking and with very little heed to the tenets of good judgment."

"And who *in your good judgment* is going to pay for that wire?"

"I expect the bank will add it to Rocking Arrow's indebtedness. Since we've picked up all the available paper, we're into them so deep, by my reckoning, they haven't much choice but to swim or sink with us, regardless."

"Anyone ever tell you you're a pretty cold fish, McGrath?"

"I don't waste much time peering into mirrors."

She said with the lips squeezed tight about her teeth, "Do you have any more of these surprises up your sleeve?"

"First thing tomorrow I figure we'll start burning off some range."

Her cheeks went white and Hardigan snarled, but before he could dump any I-told-you-sos on her, I said without beating around any bushes, "You give Rabas an inch and he'll take the whole works. You can't fiddle round to find out what he's up to—you know all you need to know about him right now. He's got his sheep pointed this way—"

"I have the feeling," she cut in, "you're a lot more involved with this man Rabas than anything we know about you can account for. Ever since you took chips in what is going on here, I've had the feeling of being in the grip of forces beyond my control or understanding. Who are you, McGrath, *and what are you up to?*"

I guess that was putting it plain enough for anyone. "Opinions and postures won't cut any parsley. As Hardigan's probably told you, I'm a convicted killer escaped from a chain gang. What you're up against here are some pretty grim facts, grimmest of which is this sheep king, Rabas. He's not going to be stopped by any ordinary methods. He's contracted to take over this whole Four Peaks country and he's just the one to do it, given half a chance. I propose to make sure he gets no chance at all and will take whatever steps appear to me to be indicated. The whys have nothing to do with you. Five shares of Rocking Arrow—as your friend Lee observed some while ago—are no guarantee against a bullet. But I'll warn you now in all fairness, ma'am, the man who takes that route to stop me had better be almighty sure of his mark."

XXII

This fetched no discernible change of expression.

The enormity of my proposal that we set fire to range in a drought-stricken country was radical enough to have fired up the tempers of persons more friendly than this pair, so I was hardly surprised at the look it produced. It might have been made to seem somewhat more palatable if I could have put former owners on land that had never belonged to them, but I had no time for such niceties and said so.

"You're not burning Turtle!" Hardigan snarled, turning ugly.

"Turtle," I told him, "will be first on the list, grass, buildings and all—including even the trees. From there we'll go to Debarra's. And when that's taken care of, we'll work back, wiping out everything between. We're not going to leave any comfort at all for—"

"You won't get away with it," Hardigan shouted. "If the bank can't stop you, I'll bring in the law!"

I grinned at him coldly. "That don't seem a heap likely. In the first place," I told him, "you won't be out of my sight, and I can't think of any law that would jump to your bidding that wouldn't be camped on my shirttail already. If you want to stay chipper, you'll bed down right here. Moving round outside once it's dark won't be healthy."

With a curt nod, I left them to find Joe unsaddling across the yard by the horse pens. I told him about the plans for tomorrow and he was quick to see the advantages of this course, but warned I had better look for trouble from Debarra. "He ain't goin' to like it one little damn bit."

"It's not Debarra I'm worried about. Make sure neither Hardigan nor Bedeler leave this place tonight.
That clear to you?"

He nodded.

I had them all in the saddle before first light. By
the time old Sol got his shine above the rim, we were
halfway to Turtle, every man jack riding with a lever
action rifle resting ready across his pommel. It was
amply evident by the ugly look on his big-nosed face
that Lee Hardigan—if he'd come to terms with my
hateful intention—was just as bitter as he'd been about
it yesterday. And no more reliable, if I correctly gauged
the glint in his stare.

I sure didn't figure to turn my back to him.

At about half a mile from Turtle's former south boundary I asked Hardigan if there was anything of value
in his house he cared to fetch. "If there is," I said,
when he refused to open his mouth, "Joe here can ride
along if you want to slip up there.

"All right, Joe," I nodded, when he still didn't answer,
"go fetch Gurley and that other feller down here."

We had a fire line to drag but after giving this a try
it seemed a lot less work and more sensible to me to
get the fires started first and drag two-three steers
across the smoldering line behind them. And this was
what we proceeded to do when Joe got back with
the two from Turtle, Hardigan working right along
with the rest of us, mad enough by his look to eat the
devil with his horns on.

There hadn't been much wind but the fire made its
own with plenty of yellowed grass here to feed on. It
took most of the morning with grueling work to keep
sparks from that blaze from taking off south across
range we had to save for the cattle I'd had moved off

Hardigan's sections. It was almost straight-up noon before we finally were ready to head for Debarra's.

"Ought to be some easier when we get over there," Joe said conversationally after we'd been a couple hours on the way. "You'll notice there's more brush an' cactus up here. Lot of rock, too, as we get nearer the rim. Salt River Canyon turns east a couple miles this side of Gourd an' Vine's north boundary an' east of that, swingin' south, there's Black River. Pretty fair chance the fire won't jump 'em."

"Then we'll cross and set more fires. The bigger the swath of range we burn, the harder it'll be for Rabas to come down on us. By my calculations, he's got somewhere in the neighborhood of two hundred and seventy thousand sheep. Don't seem reasonable he'll fetch more than one band down here. No matter how case-hardened he is, I doubt he'll be anxious to throw away ninety thousand of those blatters—which is about what it'll amount to if he tries driving those sheep across these burns."

"You think lack of feed an' water'll stop him?"

"Probably not, if that was all that stood in his way. One extra bonus we'll get from these fires is those sheep will stand out like purple camels stryin' to lope through a snow bank, and nobody'll have to point that out to him. I aim for this crew to patrol those burns. If he does try to cross, he's going to have to do it through a curtain of lead."

Joe, mulling that over, said: "Time we put the torch to Debarra's there's sure like to be one hellimonious passel of smoke an' stink blowin' round this country. Folks are like to be seein' that smoke clean to Phoenix an' Globe—mebbe even to Morenci an' Clifton. You thought about that?"

I said, "It's occurred to me. I doubt it'll fetch any great amount of lookers. If it should, we'll give out this is sheepmen's work—ought to drive a few extra nails in his coffin if he's still muleheaded enough to go on with it."

"I dunno," Joe grumbled. "This deal could raise more stink—"

"A man's got a right to protect his property—"

"If you start shootin' sheep, you'll have to shoot herders too."

"You catch a look at those fellers you'll shoot, all right. Make no mistake about that. We'll shoot or those Yaquis'll bury the lot of us! Two rules is all Rabas ever hands down. *Feed my sheep!* and *No dead ever get up in a court!*" I said to him bleakly: "How much talking did Wilbur do after that sheep crowd went through here last year?"

Hardigan, who had dropped back to put his oar in, declared with a rasp rough edge to his words: "That wasn't done in cold blood like this slaughter you're hatchin'!"

"There won't *be* any slaughter if he uses his head. Whole point of this burning is to persuade him to use it."

Hardigan sneered. "That's the stamp you put on it. Let's see what Debarra says. He won't be caught short the way you done me. He'll have four hands with guns to stand back of him!"

I felt like knocking the teeth down his throat, but just the same his talk and cur-dog looks kept nibbling away at the guy ropes of my confidence. I might hide this from the rest of the crew but I could not conceal from my own grim knowledge the shifty sand I had under me here.

He might not have the guts to openly cross me but if he kept up that kind of chin music he could sow enough doubts to cause big trouble. In a bind, without the whole support of this crew, I could damn quick wind up strumming a harp. If they hung fire when I needed and was forced to depend on them, it could give that damned Rabas sufficient encouragement to throw his whole weight against our flimsy defenses. We'd be spread damn thin despite the mobility I'd figured to count on if we were forced to patrol the whole north line of Rocking Arrow's new boundary.

And there was Shannon to reckon with. He might consider my efforts too tame for his purpose or blow up when he saw what course I was taking to implement what I'd been sent here to do. If the bluff I was running turned Rabas back, I could no longer count on the major's influence to keep the law fenced out of this Basin.

I was on borrowed time and the weight of this was hung round my neck as grimly remindful as the Mariner's albatross. In this fight for the Basin I was not a free agent. I could act like one on the choice I'd been given, but only so long as the course of events met with Shannon's approval. And walking this tightrope of bluff within bluff, I had only to make one miscalculation to have the whole house of cards fall in on me.

XXIII

"The bank," Hardigan declaimed with his lip stuck out, "will have somethin' to say about burnin' up property they've got a lien—"

"If Debarra," I said, "deals himself out of this account of anything you do or say, you better dig for the tules on the fastest nag you can fling a leg over. Now get back where you were or I'll not be responsible for any of your parts that get put out of kilter."

He bared his gums and looked meaner by God than

a new-sheared sheep, but that was far as bravado would take him. I felt sorry for the horse when, raking spurs across it, he took off with gritted teeth for the lead pair of riders, one of which was Bedeler.

Joe, looking after him, shook his head. "You'll have to climb that jigger before you're much older. Way he swells up one of these times he'll boil right over."

"When that time comes I'll probably kill the son of a bitch!"

Joe, after a look at my face, shut his mouth and we rode after that in a kind of strained silence through which the grumbling of Hardigan's tones drifted back like the rumble of distant thunder. This irritated me worse than the ache of my arm with its promise of a forthcoming storm building up, but talk wouldn't cure it. That was goddam sure.

The shank of the afternoon was well advanced when we finally sighted Debarra's headquarters perhaps a mile south of Haystack Butte. What cattle we saw there were in much better shape than the stock farther south. He had two rivers to slake their thirst and a lot of mesquite to supplement the nourishment of what grass was available, some taller here and not near as parched as the grama found in the poorer range given over to greasysack spreads we'd encountered along the way.

I had the erstwhile owners of those outfits with me when, twelve strong, we presently drew rein in Debarra's yard. He stepped from the house with a welcoming smile that became somewhat strained when he observed our condition and clamp-jawed looks. "A fire?" he said.

There was no easy way to explain what we'd come for, nor was the situation eased by Hardigan's glower and the malice so plain on Bedeler's face.

I told him soberly, "We've been burning off range to hold back the sheep. It's a hell of a thing but the only way we stand any chance to stop Rabas. Tomorrow we'll have to burn off some of yours, including," I said reluctantly, "your buildings," and saw cold shock stiffen the planes of his cheeks.

He could hardly have expected with me for a ramrod to get through this deal without some kind of sacrifice. He may not have smelled any powdersmoke on me but must have known my way would not embrace parlor socials, for the life I'd been leading left ineradicable marks that could not have escaped a man of his persuasions.

He stood, scarce breathing, another long moment with his unseeing stare frozen onto my cheeks, fists clenched at his sides and with his thoughts by the look darting this way and that, trying to make up his mind if this were one further sample of gringo chicanery.

Without a word, then, he turned and went back in the house. I stepped out of the saddle—not a graceful performance with one arm in a sling—and a glance raked across the still mounted crew showed Hardigan and Bedeler with their heads together, muttering.

I was tired and stiff and filled with testy notions or I might have thought twice about putting this off with those two cooking up something out of hearing. But Debarra, I reckoned, ought to have a little time to think over what I'd told him and get used to the idea. If I tried to force the issue and burn this place at once, with tempers short like they were, this whole deal might go up in the crash and slam of gunfire.

"We'll spend the night," I told them. Saddles skreaked as men got down and Bedeler's big frame turned toward the house as Hardigan, both their horses in tow, came after the others that were following me toward the circular pens built of mesquite posts lashed together with rawhide.

Peering across my shoulder, I watched Bedeler step

onto the porch and slip into the house, strongly minded to go after him. I was pretty near certain whatever was brewing he had been put up to, nor did I need three guesses as to whose devious mind had conceived this dido. But it occurred to me also the whole point of the maneuver could have been to get me out of the way long enough for Hardigan to set up whatever props his concealed purpose called for.

Perhaps all he wanted was the chance to take off or work out something maybe that involved my horse. It seemed a heap more likely as I pushed it around they'd got something rigged up to cook my goose with Debarra.

I got the rig off my mount and turned him into the nearest empty pen, the sounds of unsaddling mixed with thoughts that were buzzing and circling like a batch of riled hornets. The men, when I eyed them after putting up the bars, seemed a little too closely grouped for casual placement—in a kind of half circle that could have been intended to fence me in.

Joe, next to Hardigan, held a spread fingered hand not over six inches from the butt of his hip-slung colt's. He had his mouth tightly pressed across locked teeth and above that eagle's beak of a nose the rancher's flushed cheeks were livid with fury.

Jerking my chin, I pushed through the men with uncaring elbows. No foolhardy hand reached out to stop me. When I'd put some distance between myself and the pens I turned and waited for the segundo to join me. "What was that all about?"

"I dunno," Joe said. "I just didn't like the way it stacked up with that bunch of scissorsbills hemmin' you in."

"I've a hunch they figured I'd go tearing after Bedeler."

"Mebbe you should. I don't reckon he's over there to spread any oil over troubled water."

"It ain't in Debarra to trust either one of them." I put a grin on my face. "We wouldn't want to cramp the man's style would we, Joseph?"

"By God, that Hardigan's sure up to somethin'!"

"Hunting an angle. I don't think—up to now—he's got hold of one that suits him."

I'd no reason to suspect from past performance those words were due to come back and haunt me. Hardigan had had any number of chances to take a firm stand and had funked every one.

"There's some plain satisfaction," Joe growled looking past me and, following his stare, I saw the bull-necked Bedeler coming off Debarra's porch. The quirk of his jowls showed the kind of grin you'd find on a cat just coming away from a handful of feathers.

"Mex wants t' see you," he flung in my direction.

"I'll go with you," Joe offered, but I shook my head. A nebulous and somewhat contradictory notion was beginning to rub against the edge of my thinking. "Keep away from Hardigan," I said on a hunch. "If he wants to sneak a horse, let him. He's welcome to every bit of rope he can use but don't let Bedeler out of your sight."

"Ain't you got the wrong end of the glass to your eye?"

"You watch Bedeler," I said, and went over and pounded on Debarra's door. I was mildly astonished when this *puerta* opened to find confronting me a swarthy *vaquero*. A pair of filled shellbelts were looped across his open-shirted chest and his right hand was locked about the breech of a rifle.

"Where's the Indians?" I said, but those mahogany cheeks stayed ominously sober. I put away my levity. "McGrath's the monicker. I was told Don Carlos was anxious to see me."

The fellow called out something too fast to catch and like a genie another shellbelted hombre in a chin-strapped Chihuahua materialized out of an opacity of shadows. I wondered would he vanish if I clapped my hands?

With a finger through the trigger guard of a Winchester .73 he beckoned me after him, down a flagged hall. "These way, señor."

And thus I came to the room where Debarra stood waiting behind an elegant desk of some reddish wood which may have been cherry. "Forgive me the rudeness of so obnoxious a courier. It seemed discreet to allow him the pleasure of imagining I was gullible enough to believe his every word. As a matter of fact," he thinly smiled, "Bedeler's lies but confirmed suspicions I have cherished overlong with regard to your countrymen."

"That the only good Anglo was a dead one?"

"Close enough." I saw the shrewd twinkle that looked out of his stare. "I've decided, McGrath, to let you go ahead with this. In view of what that oaf had to say, I presume you could do with a little help. Do you think we had better get on with it tonight?"

I couldn't tell if he were pulling my leg. Even a reasonable man, I thought distrustfully, ought to be more worked up about the prospect of seeing his home reduced to mounds of stinking rubble.

"I expect it can wait until morning," I said. "Have you any idea how much of your stuff is spread out right now between here and the Rim?"

He spread his hands in the Mexican fashion. "I am not very efficient, I'm afraid, by Yankee standards. Still, I would hardly care to see them roasted alive. With your permission—"

"We'll get them out first thing in the morning. You mind saying what exactly Bedeler was urging?"

"It was not too clear." Debarra said: "Most of his tirade was leveled at you. He did appear to feel the bank should be notified before burning over any more of this range. I think he wanted I should hold out for that. As between you and him—or that Turtle man Hardigan, I'm inclined to believe you represent our last hope."

This was what a man would want to hear, but it didn't sound natural coming from him. "I saw two of your men as I came though the hall. Where are the other pair of Gourd and Vine hands?"

"I've sent one to Seneca to see what talk's going around. Rodriguez is watching the road through the Pass."

A smart precaution, that last, I thought grimly, but noticed he did not ask if this suited the man who was supposed to be running this syndicate deal.

XXIV

Stuffed with meat and refried frijoles, like most of the crew I turned in early, not honestly expecting to get much rest with a headful of things that had to be seen to—not to mention the worries stemmed from this thing and that.

Perhaps I was more used up than a man likes admitting. I have no remembrance of twisting and turning once stashed in my soogans, removed far enough from the rest of those yahoos to have some prospect of surviving the night. Sure, I thought some of Charlie, Hardigan and Bedeler as I lay staring up at the green wink of stars, half minded to listen for Hardigan's departure, wondering how far he'd run the rope we had loaned him.

A man can be self-seeking, as he was, and still considerably surprise by his actions those who would think to have known him best. I couldn't see that he had very much to gain—which always I'd have said would be his first consideration—by entering into any tribal rites with Rabas.

I closed my eyes and someone, next thing I knew, had hold of my shoulder and appeared to be trying to shake me loose of it. But none of this—including Joe's excited tones—seemed to make much sense until my jerked-open stare caught the gray drift of shapes pressing steadily past in the roundabout dark. I latched onto things then. Knew what I'd been hearing was not phantom sounds out of some hateful dream.

"What's the time?" I snarled, throwing off Joe's hand to struggle upright, but wasn't able to make out what he said through the bedlam of bleating stupid damned sheep being crammed into the yard like sardines all about us. Vaguely back of this uproar I was conscious of shouts and cursing, and yet, strangely enough, no bang and thump of spitting guns.

It seemed already to be lighter in the east and in the lifting wind there was the feel of rain as I pushed Joe impatiently toward the house. "Where's Hardigan?" I mouthed against the side of his head as we beat and battered a path through the wool greasy smell of this blatting hoard.

The only word I could catch to be sure of was *gone*, and that sure as hell figured though I still couldn't savvy how a gent playing angles, and already fixed to travel in double harness with the fattest lump of stock a man could put together, could hope to do half as good rubbing knees so to speak with a hombre as hungry as this profit minded Rabas.

Yet . . . where else would he have gone?

It was too much coincidence to swallow to believe these sheep had just happened to descend on Debarra a bare handful of hours before we were set to burn off the cover. Somebody had to have warned Rabas some-how.

He might have had flankers out, point men or foragers . . . or one of these two-bit owners who had not been invited or—like Giles—had refused to come under the Rocking Arrow umbrella could have carried him word of the burning at Turtle.

Sure, I'd thought all along he would likely come this way, that his buying of Boxed O was a kind of red herring set up to mislead with its obvious threat the cow crowd's attention.

It was the timing of this arrival, the rapier thrust so close on the heels of Hardigan's departure, which so bitterly underscored my failure to realize how far he'd go in his spleen to unhorse me.

What had happened to the man Debarra'd sent to watch the Pass?

But a lot more urgent among the pressures put on me by Rabas' coup was what to do now. How much of the original plan could we salvage? How much of the syndicate lands could we save? Rabas' takeover here, where there still was good forage, had dealt a bad blow to my confidence and to what bleak chance we might still have to whip him.

No half measures could be depended on now. Unless we could turn these sheep back, and soon, we might just as well yell calf rope and quit.

I went into the house, Joe hard on my heels, but someone I reckoned had better round up the crew. I gave him that chore, spun him round, shoved him door-ward. "And get the gear on our horses. Have the boys ready to ride inside of ten minutes!"

I went on to find Debarra glumly drinking in his sala. He waved a mock nonchalant hand at the bottle but I growled, "That's not the answer. We're bent pretty bad but we're not whipped yet. They've stolen a march and won the first skirmish. It's our move now and we had better get at it."

"What can we do?" Debarra looked pretty down.

"We'll do what we set out to do. Burn off your range."

The old Don looked shocked. He pawed at his face. "Man, you can't!"

"You'll damn soon see— Come along," I growled, and he caught hold of my arm. "But my cattle!" he cried.

"You'll lose some, I guess, but they're not your worry anyway. They belong to Rocking Arrow. Most of 'em will take off soon's they smell smoke and get a look at those flames. They'll go hightailing it right through Rabas' camp and he'll lose enough sheep—"

"But I have *things* in this house!"

There wasn't time to argue. Every wasted minute was putting those sheep deeper into range Rocking Arrow had to have if we were going to survive these burnings and a drought which had already drastically curtailed the supply of feed.

I reached the main entrance, hauled open the door and heard the old man, still grumbling, coming down the flagged hall. I called with some impatience, "Where are those two hombres—"

"I sent them out to keep an eye on the horses. Can't you give me an hour—"

I went through the door and was half across the porch before I properly noticed the shapes of mounted men looming wraithlike above that bleating river of sheep. In the disorganized state of my emotions at the moment I took them for Yaquis and would certainly have emptied two-three saddles had not Joe just then loosed a warning shout.

I said, bringing the hand away from my hip, "They all here but Hardigan?" It appeared that they were— fifteen of us in all, including the pair of big-hatted hombres I had seen in Debarra's house earlier on. I sent the nearest after Debarra and both—when finally they came staggering out—held great armfuls of stuff the old man, apparently, could not bring himself to part with.

By that time, you bet, I was plumb out of patience.

"You can drop that crap right there," I said bluntly. "This ain't no box social we're headed for—"

"But these pictures, señor, are my ancestors!"

We could jaw here all night. "Let's go!" I snarled, slamming my horse around, pointing him south same as the sheep that would not get out of our way for sour apples. "Shoot me a path through those stupid damn sheep!" I yelled at Joe, furious, and he emptied his Winchester over their heads.

They did spread out some, three or four leaping over the backs of those nearest, but it took swinging ropes' ends to force enough leeway to buck horses through.

I thought on my soul we'd never get clear of them. In this brightening light as far as we could see up ahead there were sheep spread over this county like a dirty gray blanket. They were still being pushed from somewhere far back, but after an hour of leadfooted progress they began to thin out up ahead and fifteen minutes later we were through them and clear of their stench and their yammer.

"Start shooting," I yelled. "If they won't turn, pile 'em up!"

"You'll never stop them that way—it didn't stop them last year," Bedeler called, standing up in his stirrups.

"What's that stuff?" I growled, catching hold of Debarra's man Friday who still had his arms filled with rolls of what looked to be brocaded cloth. Debarra came panting up as I jerked a couple of the rolls away. "Take care—" he cried, "they're old tapestries! Priceless!"

Whirling my horse as several of the crew began knocking down the nearing bellwethers I drove in the steel and put a quarter of a mile between myself and the infuriated old man. I could still hear him shouting as he ran for his mount. He had already lost all but one of his "ancestors" so I couldn't too much blame him for being in a temper.

But this was no time for sentiment. I tied the end of my rope to one squeezed-together corner of each of his heirlooms, shook them out and put a match to the opposite ends. Bone dry with the years, both burst into flame. Paying out rope, I raced my mount with this flaming drag hellity larrup across the browse, out in front of those oncoming woolies.

Debarra—in the van of the hurrying crew—burst out of the smoke at a headlong gallop, stopping his horse in a rearing slide not ten feet away, soot-streaked livid features convulsed with a splutter and passion he couldn't find words for. You'd have thought the old man was on the verge of a stroke.

Confused, bewildered and trapped in the mounting pressure from those massed sheep behind, the flock's leaders, terrified, suddenly broke and went pounding away on either flank in blind panic. But churning hooves were no match for the express train speed of that wind driven wall of leaping flames.

XXV

It took us better than an hour to get the south rim of that burn stomped out, even after relays of drags killed the worst of it. We were still on Gourd and Vine range but only just barely, with scarcely a mile of its grass left intact.

Debarra, when I finally found chance to talk with the man, looked considerably shaken. But most of his rage had been whittled away in the sights and sounds we had all of us come through. He wore a look now of stunned resignation. "There was nothing else," I said, "we could do that stood any chance of stopping that bastard. God knows I'm not proud of that—doubt I'll ever get the stink off me, but somebody had to prove we mean business. I don't know how many sheep got cooked in that fire but whatever their number it's a damn sight more than they figured to lose."

Debarra just looked at me, shaking his head.

"If you don't have the stomach for this kind of thing—" I testily started when Joe, peering south, grumbled, "Horse in a hurry!" and grabbed up his saddle gun. But it was only one man and I'd made out it was coosie before someone back of me disgustedly grunted, "Rittenhouse."

Cook's bulged stare took in the dark lumps that strewed the charred path of the holocaust I'd loosed. He pawed at his face as though about to be sick. To head him off I asked, gruffly curt: "Conrado have any word for me?"

"He sure will when he hears about this. Bank's real unhappy about that burnin' at Turtle—"

"How the hell would they hear of that before you quit town?"

"Hardigan rode in—I didn't leave till this mornin'— was waitin' on that wire. Locked in the warehouse an' when it opened up they wouldn't let me hev it. Said the bank had sent word our order had been cancelled!"

Never send a boy I thought, and realized then it didn't make no great world of difference if they had refused to put up the money. Knowing it was there, we could ride in and take the stuff; I guessed we had better be about it pronto. Then I thought, *What the hell!* With the kind of loss we had just dumped on Rabas, it wasn't hardly likely we'd have call for any wire.

I sent Bedeler and one of the hands that had suffered minor burns back with coosie, to be with Kay Wilbur just in case. I didn't reckon she'd need them but I didn't either, which goes to show I was more shook up by this killing and burning than most folks would figure. Including myself.

There had to be some reason I wasn't thinking straight. Anybody who'd uncovered all the things I had about Rabas had no business taking anything for granted.

Joe groused: "Who the hell's side is that bank on anyhow?"

I slanched a look at the sky, wondering what had happened to that rain I'd smelled last night. Reckoned the wind must have dumped it someplace north of the Mogollon Rim—there sure hadn't none of it come down here. Which was likely just as well, considering our need of that blaze I'd sent Rabas.

"Maybe," I said, "they figure I'm too hard on their prospects. Probably don't fancy having it get round they've been picking up the bills of a feller so casual about playing with matches."

But Joe was the only one who grinned back at me. Debarra said, "They can't close us out for our indebtedness, can they?"

"Not a heap likely so long as we don't fall behind on the interest."

But I was just talking off the top of my head. Who was to say what a small cow country bank might not do? A new, harder thought was flopping round through my head. Smarter gents than myself had been diddled by slick talking bankers. With Hardigan up there yapping his head off, it was dollars to doughnuts they would seize any halfway reasonable chance to cut loose of me.

I didn't think Hardigan had the kind of money to make a worthwhile offer, but Rabas had certainly. What if he had bought up our notes or was about to? Bad as we must have hurt him with that fire, I'd been too ready to write the man off, forgetting that in this he wasn't a free agent. He'd be acting—according to Shannon's calculations—for the combine trying to smash Roosevelt's Forest and Park bills. He *couldn't* pull out under that kind of pressure. No matter how bad we'd hurt him.

I tried to put myself in his boots, to think as he'd think and come up with a solution. Why take more risks when he had capital enough to wreck that bank? Hell, he wouldn't even need to buy up our notes—a big enough deposit and a few well chosen threats. . . .

I called Joe aside. "I'm going in to have a talk with that banker. You take these boys and go on like we planned, connecting up this burn with the one over at Turtle. We've got to destroy enough browse to make Rabas think twice before risking more— Wait! Never mind that." I took hold of his arm. "We can hurt him worse if we just hold back and catch him again like we did right here. Means we'll have to patrol this whole line, unless—

"Tell you what. Put a couple boys on a pair of these buttes farther north to watch out for him. Rest of you stay bunched. Then whichever one spots him can send up a smoke and you can take the whole crew in that direction. Don't start another fire till you see the sheep. Then make damn sure they don't get past. Next time maybe he'll have those Yaquis out in front, so watch yourselves. Sheep or Yaquis, you wait till you see them before you touch off any more of this range. Got it?"

"Right."

THE TEXAS GUN

. It was well after dark when I rode into Sunflower but the town very obviously hadn't yet gone to bed. The bank and most of the stores were closed but there was plenty of traffic along Saloon Row.

I stopped by the marshal's office but the redheaded Durphey wasn't holding down his desk—probably, I thought, out making his rounds. Might even be smarter if I kept plumb away because if Shannon didn't like the way things were going, the marshal might have orders to pick me up on sight. I'd likely get just as far as Conrado anyway. If the lawyer refused to back my hand we could get more mileage from the press than from Red Durphey.

Conrado's office was dark but the Sunflower *Bugle* was lit up like a Christmas tree. Leaving my horse at the rack, I went into the empty front office, rounded the counter and moved into the pressroom where an ink-smeared devil was working over the stone. At a desk nearby, under a hanging lamp, a crotchety looking old geezer in a green eyeshade was bent over a stack of galleys.

"Is the proprietor around?" I asked of this hombre. Without looking up he said, "Who wants to know?"

"Just tell him Pete McGrath dropped by en route from a die-up and burning at Debarra's."

That fetched his head up. He gave me a sharp look over his spectacles. "Keep talkin'," he grumbled. I shook my head at him.

"Whatever you've heard, that story ain't half of it. The whole Four Peaks country is up in arms, mister. Turtle's been burned—"

"At your orders, I'm told. Wasn't that kind of drastic?"

"Not if you want to keep this country for cattle."

"Who burned out Debarra?"

"You're looking right at him."

"You've the guts to admit it?"

143

"We're not playing parlor games!" I told him about Kay Wilbur turning Rocking Arrow into a syndicate. "She kind of figured," I said, "as the biggest outfit, the least she could do with those sheep pointed this way was put out a helping hand to her neighbors."

The man said skeptically, "By the terms of this deal, according to your tell, she didn't hurt herself none picking up that extra range and giving those boobs a stake in the outfit. She stands, if you lose, to pull the whole bunch under, but with all of them knowin' this maybe she'll manage to come out on top if she can keep you from burnin' up the whole damn country."

I expect my words had a kind of rough edge when I asked if he knew any better way to keep sheep out of a cowman's kitchen.

"How many sheep do you reckon was trapped in that fire?"

"I'd guess anyway several hundred."

"There was ninety thousand in the batch those Yaquis put through Carrizo on their way to the Salt. If the wind was right you may have bagged the whole works."

"He'll have to be hurt worse than that to be stopped." I mentioned the combine the sheep and lumber interests had put together in their efforts to defeat the President's National Forests bill. "There's a heap of money behind this feller, and a heap of pressure. Someone had to tell him what we were up to, for those sheep to hit Debarra before we were set."

"So?"

"Could be someone's trading secrets for cash."

Maybe it was the tone of my words that turned his eyes to watchful slits. As though trying it for sound he said, "You figure to take him out of the play."

When that brought nothing, he made a few jots on the back of a galley, looked up in that studying way at me again. "You wanta name names?"

It didn't seem—if Hardigan had indeed been to the bank—he could have taken time out enough to get in touch with Rabas, but Conrado had all the time in the world and knew my plans from A to izzard. He didn't even have to see or speak; could have sent someone else. The only thing I hadn't put on his plate was a timetable.

And I told myself anyone could be bought if the price was right . . . the way Charlie had bought that San Saba banker.

I ran my tongue across lips that were hot for revenge. "Not yet," I said. "You got a handle?"

"MacIntosh. You've made some pretty hefty statements—"

"You'll get no affidavits . . . be a lot more like to get yourself killed, but I'll put you where you can pick your own names if you'll say where I can find Conrado real quick."

"You wouldn't kid a man would you?"

"Why don't you come along with me now and find out?"

XXVI

Conrado lived in the Nob Hill section in a gingerbready mansion heired from his father who—Mac said —had once been connected with mines in the vicinity. It never occurred to me to ask what kind, copper being prevalent all through these mountains. I was a sight more interested in pinning down the leak which had permitted us to come within an ace of being euchred by the untimely arrival of Rabas' sheep at Gourd and Vine.

Unless this hole was plugged, we would all of us have

to hike like hell just to stay at where we were right now.

"I don't see what you hope to get out of this," MacIntosh grumbled, as we sat in his rig outside the place. "If this feller's your man, he'd hardly be foolish enough to admit it. We can't beat it out of—"

"Speak for yourself." At least the lawyer was home, more than I'd looked for I reminded myself as we sat bleakly peering at a lamplighted window. "You reckon anybody's with him?"

"Now that I think of it, this was his lodge night. If he'd gone—he generally does—he wouldn't be home yet."

Speculation wasn't apt to put much porridge on our plates. I hauled the pistol from my belt, fingered the holes and shoved it back, making sure it lay loose in easy grabbing position. "You coming?" I asked, getting out to glance back at him.

He wrapped the reins round the whipstock with somewhat less than a newshound's enthusiasm. I said, "Don't feel like you got to. This might turn out to be more than you bargained for. More especial if he's got someone else up there with him."

"You mean like . . . Rabas?"

His eyes stood out like two knots on a stick. I gave his foolish question the amount of answer it deserved, vaulted lightly over the shut spring gate in the white picket fence and went up the path to bang at the door with the brass horsehead knocker.

The fanlight brightened with the sound of an approaching tread and MacIntosh, bidding better judgment goodbye, loped up as the door opened, to push through on my heels.

"Well," Conrado exclaimed, hoisting his lamp the better to see, "this *is* a surprise. To what do I owe—"

"Just put on your hat and come along," I said, catching his lamp holding arm by the elbow. "We're craving a talk with your friend at the bank. Don't waste time with a lot of fancy rhetoric."

You could see he didn't much care for the program but could tell by the feel of my grip on his arm he hadn't a great deal of choice. With cheeks showing stiff, he set down the lamp and, putting the best face he could on the matter, took up his hat from the mahogany tree. As we moved down the path he said to me dryly: "If I'd known when we started as much about you as I learned last night—"

"What's happened to make Lee Hardigan look so much better than he did when you told me his old man was hanged for a horse thief?"

Through flattened lips, with contempt in his tone, Conrado answered the question, lawyer fashion, with another. "Aren't you acting pretty brash for a man so recently escaped from a chain gang?"

We both heard the gasp this jerked out of Mac. While I was feeling the edge of the man's narrowed stare, Conrado—quick to broaden any crack of advantage—said, like a judge about to hand down a sentence: "Does that imply you didn't know you've been carting round a convicted murderer? Has this killer's glib tongue taken *you* in, too?"

I loosed a harsh laugh. "You're wasting good breath if you're scratching for ethics or conscience in the fourth estate. The man's after a story and the one he'll come up with is going to rock this country from one end to the other. Better ask yourself, Conrado, how it happens the sheriffs and marshals haven't already nailed me if that gab Hardigan's spreading isn't cut from whole cloth."

I don't know if that shook him but he got into the buggy without further talk. Mac climbed aboard on the other side and when I joined them, picked up the reins. "Claibourn's home I suppose?"

"Well," said Conrado, "he's not very likely to be at the bank."

The man was home and still up. He looked a mite astonished to find our faces peering back from his doorstep. I shoved forward the reluctant lawyer, stepped in after him and made room for Mac who pushed the door to and put his shoulders against it. "You know these 'gents," I said to the banker. "My name's Mc-Grath. We've come here with questions that need some straight answers."

"If it's bank business—" he started, blowing up his chest.

"You called the turn first pop from the box, and it ain't the sort of thing that can wait till tomorrow. Has your bank got Rabas' name on its books?"

For a man in shirtsleeves and carpet slippers with eight long hairs combed across his bald head, he did pretty well in his attempt at affronted dignity. Before his splutter could be properly unleashed, I said sharply blunt: "You can make this as hard on yourself as you want to but we're not clearing out till we've got what we came for. A quick yes or no will save a lot of bruised feelings. I'm asking just once more: Does Rabas have an account with your bank?"

"No," he said after licking his lips.

"Do you still have the Rocking Arrow notes in your vault?"

The banker turned a little pale around the gills.

"This feller plays rough," Conrado said. "You better tell him."

"As a matter of fact I do," Claibourn said. "But if you came here figuring to take them away—"

"Has Rabas done any business at all with you?"

"No."

"Would you know him if you saw him?"

"Yes . . ." Claibourn said, and wet his lips to growl

nervously, "he stopped in last fall to cash a check when he went through."

"Have you seen him since?"

"No."

Sweat showed on his jowls as I continued to eye him. "It's the truth, God damn it!" he irascibly shouted. "What does a man have to do to convince you?"

"If you haven't had any conversation with Rabas or one of his hirelings, why did you refuse to pay for that wire?"

"Because your outfit is into us deep enough already. If that sheepman takes over, we'll be lucky to survive the loans we've made now."

"Then I'd think you'd want to make sure he wasn't able."

"I've got a board of directors—"

"Now we're getting somewhere. You okayed that wire when Conrado brought it up with you, after which somebody, catching wind of this, started flinging their weight around." I put more steel in my look. "How much sheep money is on deposit in your bank?"

Claibourn tried bluster but it was plain he was hedging when he declared with too much emphasis, "Not a cent of Rabas' money's ever passed through our—"

"To hell with Rabas! Who's money is it that changed your mind about that wire?"

"It will take a court order—"

"Never mind," I said. "We've found out what we came for." I shoved Mac aside and pulled open the door. I said over my shoulder, "You can read about yourself playing footsie with sheepmen when this whole deal gets spilled across the pages of the *Bugle*."

"Here—wait!" he cried, shaken, but what was there to wait for? I reckoned it was Hardigan had someway fetched those sheep after all. It still didn't look to make good sense for him to sell out his neighbors and the

girl to boot, but it appeared from here he'd had a
damn good try. Probably come straight for town after
quitting Debarra's but that didn't prove his hand wasn't
in it. He could have sent Rabas word. By Giles or some
other dissatisfied clown.

We bade Conrado good night in front of his house. I
had Claibourn pegged for a typical mealy-mouthed
banker. But I wasn't the only one thinking about him.
Just before we pulled up in front of his office, "You
know," Mac said, "you've got that feller scared pissless."

"Do him good. Maybe it will teach him not to suck
eggs. What kind of mining was Conrado's old man
mixed up with?"

"Copper most of the time, though he poked around
some on an amethyst vein that pinched out about the
time he was due to cash in."

"Didn't suppose there was any of that around here."

"Had a pretty good thing going there for awhile. Old
Wilbur found an outcrop on his place two-three months
before his clash with Rabas put an end to him. Girl
had it looked at. Just a shallow pocket not commercially
profitable—"

"Says who?"

"Why that minin' feller Hardigan fetched in for her."

"Was his father a cowhand?"

"Hardigan's? Sure. What time he worked at it. Spent
most of his time moving other folks' horses."

"He ever work for Wilbur?"

"Not that I know of. He was on Boxed O, where old
Conrado had been gopherin' for amethyst, when he
got that horse kicked out from under him."

A kind of halfway notion was digging itself out at
the edge of my mind and I stepped down from the
buggy still wooling it around. Hardigan's backing and
filling just might make a heap more sense than I'd

figured. Suppose, for some reason, Kay had changed her mind about spending the rest of her life spliced to him. . . .

I was by my horse, reaching down for the reins I had wrapped round the tie pole, when the marshal, Red Durphey, stepped out of the shadows. "Guess you ain't quite as bright as you been cracked up to be," he said round his chaw in an odd tone of voice.

"What's that supposed to mean?"

"Means while you been hobnobbin' with lawyers and bankers, Rabas an' his Injuns bypassed your crew, took over Boxed O and are pushin' more sheep hard an' fast straight for Wilbur's!"

XXVII

It figured.

When you send a boy to take over your work there's no one to blame but yourself if he fizzles. Joe, like enough, done the best he could. He hadn't the age or the savvy to come off well in anything requiring him to outguess Rabas. I should have thought about this before trusting the fate of this whole Basin country to folks who'd been licked once by Rabas already.

Mac, at my elbow, growled, "What can you do?"

"What I reckoned to have to do when I got into this—"

"An hour late," gruffed Durphey, disgusted. "For what chance you've got I wouldn't give a thin dime. They'll sheep every cowman out of this country!"

"I ain't noticed you doing no bleeding for anything."

With a cold sneer. Durphey turned on his heel. The clank of his spurs dribbled out in the distance.

He had only been echoing what Shannon, no doubt,

had more strongly said. A wonder, I thought, he hadn't put cuffs on me. Sure wasn't my busted wing that had stopped him.

Beside me Mac said, "I guess they're washin' their hands of you."

It pulled round my head to stare at him sharply. With a wry sort of grin he put a hand on my shoulder. "I can still get four from totin' two and carrying two. If you're the McGrath killed that San Saba banker it don't take no gypsy cards for a man quick as me to savvy how come the law's not caught up with you. If I come up with fresh horses can we beat 'em to Wilbur's?"

"We can damn well try!"

With two mounts apiece, cutting straight as the contour of tumbled hills would let us, we must have been nearer than halfway to the home place when—stopped again to change horses—Mac said abruptly, "You hear anything?"

"Somebody back of us. Durphey—maybe Shannon."

"Come to lend us a hand, you reckon?"

"Ain't you grown out of Santa Claus yet?"

"What else would they come for?"

"To bury or jail me. Whichever seems indicated."

He finished cinching up, got hold of the tow rope and got aboard. "You got the sound of a man who doesn't care which."

"I care," I grunted, and we ran south again. To now there'd been no sign of the sheep, but since they'd have started from another direction, this was no guarantee we'd got past or ahead of them.

Durphey's tell—while almost certainly correct—did not have to be accurate in all of its details. Any number of things might have held up the drive or delayed its advance from their base at Boxed O. Joe may have guessed he'd been played for a sucker and taken the crew over there or to Turtle. But Rabas' bunch would have been watching for that; it just wasn't in the cards he'd be able to stop them.

"So what do we do?" Mac spoke up at last.

"Cut off a snake's head and the rest doesn't matter. We'll wait at the ranch if they don't beat us to it."

"You really think he's moving in with those sheep?"

When that didn't buy anything he said, rather wistful, "You figure to duel it out with him?"

"Does it look like to you I been cut out for a hero? Crissake, Mac!"

"You mean you aim to start shooting soon as you see him?"

"I'm not going out there to play Robin Hood."

"Man, they'll *hang* you the next time!"

"Doubt there'll be enough left for that. Try adding it up. You ever hear of Rabas going anyplace without Charlie Ostermann right at his heels? That's two guns against me, plus maybe some Yaquis. And if I've got this pegged right, you'll see Hardigan siding him."

"That doesn't," Mac said, "leave much room for error."

He said more hopefully, "Marshal's probably fetchin' a posse. When he sees what a bind you're—"

"He knew what I'd have to do before I left town. He used just the right words. Never wasted a breath. But sooner or later I'd have got to this anyway."

"To a shoot-out, you mean?"

"The old gun down. Yep." The Rocking Arrow yard was just ahead of us now. In plain sight but not empty. Bedeler was there, benched outside the cookshack, and the feller I'd sent back with burns from Debarra's. I didn't notice no smoke coming out of the stovepipe but coosie's Dutch oven was bedded in coals and in this gray early light I could see him bent over it, pothook in hand gone suddenly motionless as his face came around for a look across his shoulder.

"I reckon he's got on enough to include you, only right now we're not taking time out to eat it. You head for the house and don't give me no argument. You're all I can spare to look out for those women—"

"I didn't spend half the night ridin' to get here—"

"Just do what I tell you. If it's the story you're sweating you can get it from there. Here—" I said, cutting off argument, "take these nags with you."

Coming out of the stirrup, I waved a beckon at the three by the cookshack. Cook dropped his pothook and came on the double, the burnt hand right after him. Bedeler, scowling, finally got off his ass.

"Coosie," I said—it was easier than Rittenhouse—"Rabas has jumped Boxed O and is pushing this way with another bunch of sheep. They could show any moment—probably this time they'll have some men out in front. I want you boys to catch up your saddle guns, get dug in someplace where you can make sure they get a warm welcome. *Don't fire before I do.* Go on now, get set."

I could pretty well guess what was in Bedeler's head but I went on toward the shack, picked up a tin cup and poured me some java. Mr. Arbuckle's best. The only spare rifle I could locate was an old lever action Henry, sixteen shots, with the magazine full and one charge in the chamber. This was not the best gun in the world but it would do if my hand gun ran empty before the slug with my name on it found me.

Toting this and my coffee—rather clumsily to be sure —I looked around for a good place to greet them. Of the limited choices suitable to my purpose, it looked like the best was the one Bedeler had warmed, the bench set against the front wall of the cookshack. As I was making toward this, Kay Wilbur called my name from the gallery.

"Not now," I said and, leaning the rifle within easy reach, sat down on the bench, freed my six-shooter and thrust it, butt up, on the bench between legs. "Everybody out of sight—*muy pronto.*"

Kay had her mouth open but Mac got her someway back into the house. I took a swig of my coffee and sat there holding the cup in my hands. This was women's work—waiting. I didn't know where Bedeler had got and didn't much care so long as he held back the treacherous shout he figured to tip Rabas' bunch off with until the visiting committee got in range of my pistol.

Matter of fact, I *wanted* that shout for the distractionary effect it could have on whoever came into this yard, affording the split seconds I would need to get the gun up in line and trigger that gut shot I'd promised myself when first I'd took off to hunt down Charlie.

For once, it looked like, I'd guessed right about Rabas. The sheep king had learned his costly lesson. They drifted in from the east, gingerly walking their horses with the lift of the sun copper bright at their backs, well advanced this time from the sounds of the sheep —Rabas the last to swing into the yard.

First, by a dwindling thirty feet, came Lee Hardigan, edgily riding his oxbows, reins round the horn, both hands full of rifle. Coming up as he slowed, close behind, was Ostermann, hat pulled low, cinched on with a chin strap, the sun flashing sparkles of light from gold spurs.

In plain sight I held the cooling cup in both fists, banking on this patently awkward device to fend off the die-up till Rabas should be deep enough into the yard there'd be at least a fair chance of taking him with me.

While not being terribly obvious about it, he was certainly in no great hurry to oblige. I suppose he figured this was some kind of trick, me sitting there in plain sight and plumb solo with an old beat-up Henry a good two feet from my grab.

Hardigan, more skittish even than I was in this crawling wait for Bedeler's shout, abruptly stopped and with a snarl of nerves clapped rifle to shoulder.

"Hold it!" Rabas' growl rang out. "I want a couple words with this peckerneck before anybody makes a colander out of him!"

Pushed by his twisted boil of hate, it appeared for a second Lee was going to fire anyway: so froze to the trigger was the man's rigid shape. But, two-thirds coyote, he hadn't the stomach to openly defy that old wolf's beller. Still covering me with his unlowered piece, the hard weight of him reluctantly settled into the saddle.

Charlie Ostermann—whose expression I couldn't make out through that glare—sidestepped his mount several widths to the right to give Rabas room to steer his horse in between; which he did, coming on perhaps another dozen strides before, this much ahead of the stopped, jaw-clamped Hardigan, he pulled up to frowningly have his long look. At me trapped with that tin cup two-handedly clutched against the front of my brisket.

Didn't seem like I was going to get them any closer and—without Bedeler yelled—I hadn't a Chinaman's chance of putting a slug into anyone with Hardigan holding the drop like he was and Ostermann lynx-eyed jumpy as a kidnaped virgin waking up in a whorehouse. But it was Rabas I had to get out of Shannon's hair. . . .

Then it come to me how maybe if a lie got told big enough it might drive every last thing out of his head but the burning desire to fix my clock with his own two hands.

"Pretty rough, old man," I said to him sneery. "But

not to hold a candle to how it will get when that news-paperman writes up this deal, telling how *not one, but both* those great blattin' bands of woolies you fetched to sheep out the cowmen got fried into chitlins. Account of one fool you forgot to buy off."

"I— *That's loco!*" Rabas snarled. "You couldn't work that trick a second time! We bypassed your crew—"

"Not all of them you didn't. I hid out a few your spy didn't know about," I said through the flash of a grin at Hardigan. "What he saw at Debarra's were just the boys he could recognize; the ones I fetched in from Sunflower—compliments of that banker—was cached in the hills watching your Injuns take over Boxed O.

"No need to wait for your sheep, they won't get here. Had us another fry-up. You're ruined, old man. You ain't got no more outfit than what's right here with you."

I don't guess he more than half swallowed that but he was afraid just the same it might turn out to be true. You could see it race through him, through those little pig eyes before, cheeks livid with fury, he slammed his horse forward. "*Look out!*" Bedeler yelled; I caught up my pistol.

I wasn't a gunslinger, just an average fair hand who was scared he'd never find time for them both and ter-ribly wanted to make sure of Charlie. But a lot of folks were counting on me, people like Debarra and Gurley who had sunk their all in this fight against sheep. I owed something, too, for the faith and good will and the trust they'd put in me. Cut off a snake's head and the rest won't amount to much—that's what they said and by God it was true! I put the first shot into Rabas; whipped half around as a slug jerked my vest, and drove one at Ostermann.

But I hurried it too much, afraid time would run out,

with the whine of Hardigan's lead all around me, whacking the shack, screaming off in ricochet.

Charlie, too—though guns were his livelihood—was too much in a sweat to quit his saddle, and this frantic impulse to empty his weapon with that horse dancing under him pointed up the craziness of banging away in a fit of passion.

There was more to this trade than headlong speed. I took a deep breath and let it out. Forcing myself to take careful aim, the next shot I squeezed slammed him back in his saddle and the terrified horse bolted out from under. I drew a bead on his belly and fired once more. He came half off the ground with jaws stretched wide in a yell that never got out of his chest.

That was all there was to it. Hardigan lay with his face in the dirt. I saw Mac, with Kay, running out of the house. "You've got your story—make the most of it," I called, and pulled myself into Rabas' saddle.

"Hey! What about Shannon?"

I lifted a wave and rode out of the yard.

Nelson Nye was born in Chicago, Illinois. He was educated in schools in Ohio and Massachusetts and attended the Cincinnati Art Academy. His early journalism experience was writing publicity releases and book reviews for the *Cincinnati Times-Star* and the *Buffalo Evening News*. In 1935 he began working as a ranch hand in Texas and California and became an expert on breeding quarter horses on his own ranch outside Tucson, Arizona. Much of this love for horses can be found in exceptional novels such as *Wild Horse Shorty* and *Blood of Kings*. He published his first Western short story in *Thrilling Western* and his first Western novel in 1936. He continued from then on to write prolifically, both under his own name and the bylines Drake C. Denver and Clem Colt. During the Second World War, he served with the U.S. Army Field Artillery. In 1949–1952 he worked as horse editor for *Texas Livestock Journal*. He was one of the founding members of the Western Writers of America in 1953 and served twice as its president. His first Golden Spur Award from the Western Writers of America came to him for best Western reviewer and critic in 1954. In 1958–1962 he was frontier fiction reviewer for the *New York Times Book Review*. His second Golden Spur came for his novel *Long Run*. His virtues as an author of Western fiction include a tremendous sense of authenticity, an ability to keep the pace of a story from ever lagging, and a fecund inventiveness for plot twists and situations. Some of his finest novels have had off-trail protagonists such as *The Barber of Tubac*, and both *Not Grass Alone* and *Strawberry Roan* are notable for their outstanding female characters. His books have sold over 50,000,000 copies worldwide and have been translated into the principal European languages. The *Los Angeles Times* once praised him for his "marvelous lingo, salty humor, and real characters." Above all, a Nye Western possesses a vital energy that is both propulsive and persuasive.